MW01256801

WITCH OUT OF TIME

A BLAIR WILKES MYSTERY

ELLE ADAMS

To be notified when Elle Adams's next book is released and get a free short story, *Witch at Sea*, sign up to her author newsletter.

I stood face to face with my familiar and assumed the most authoritative tone I could muster. "Sky, please put on the hat."

Sky, a little black cat with one white paw, sat on the grassy hillside and refused to move, forcing the other witches and wizards to step around him. It was amazing how such a small cat could bring an entire procession of paranormals to a halt.

I crouched beside him and looked into his eyes—one grey, one blue. "Sky, after Saturday, you won't have to do this again. Will you please cooperate with me?"

"Miaow," he said, in tones that implied he'd rather take a nap.

Halloween—or Samhain, as it was known in the magical world—was one of the most important occasions for witches and wizards all over the country, and Madame Grey had been thrilled when Fairy Falls was selected to play host to the region's most prestigious coven leaders.

Madame Grey herself led the procession, and dozens of witches and wizards walked along the hillside, all wearing black cloaks and hats with their familiars walking at their sides. At first, I'd worried that I'd forget my hat or trip over my cloak, but it was Sky who was more likely to make a deliberate spectacle of himself.

Most of the time, Sky acted like a regular witch's familiar—except for the times he glamoured himself to look like a giant furry monster to defend me. He'd fly on a broom and help me with spells, but he would not, under any circumstances, wear a pointed hat.

"I know you're not a witch familiar," I whispered. "Just play along. It's all in good fun."

"Miaow." Sky huffed, batting at the little pointed hat with a paw and knocking it into the mud. I'd spent the better part of the last hour levitating it back onto his head every time he knocked it off during rehearsals. If I'd known we'd have to spend the last two months practising three times a week, I might have hesitated before volunteering, but the ceremony meant a great deal to Madame Grey. Since she owned the town of Fairy Falls and had gone out of her way to make me feel welcome here, the least I could do was take part.

Sky, on the other hand, had no such loyalties. I had the impression that fairy cats rarely took an interest in humans at all. Before he'd adopted me, his best friend had been Vincent, an eight-hundred-year-old vampire. But Madame Grey was adamant that every witch or wizard who had a familiar was required to bring it to take part in the ceremony. It was a freezing, drizzly October day, not ideal for trekking across the hillside, but the weather didn't bother Sky nearly as much as the idea of having to pretend to be a normal feline.

As I planted the hat on Sky's head again, my flatmate Alissa gave me a sympathetic look. Her cat, Roald, padded at her side, his own pointed hat perched on top of his ears.

"See, Roald has no problem wearing a hat," I told Sky.

"Miaow." Sky's tone suggested he didn't much care what Roald did. The other familiars didn't know quite what to make of him, but they kept a noticeable distance from him. Sky might be the size of a kitten, but I'd seen him grow into a giant man-sized monster when I was under threat.

"Maybe you should borrow another cat for the ceremony," Alissa suggested. "The familiar shop has a few they're loaning to the academy students."

"Miaow." Sky bared his teeth in warning, implying any cat who dared take his place would be sorry they stepped within five feet of me.

I narrowed my eyes back at him. "If you don't want me to bring another cat, Sky, you'll have to do as I say. I'm not a fan of the weather either, but in another week, you'll never have to wear a pointed hat again."

Around us, the procession began to move forwards. I flicked my wand and levitated the black hat onto Sky's head. He twitched, making a hissing noise, but walked at my side along the muddy hillside. The lake at the foot of the hill reflected the darkening sky, while Fairy Falls itself was visible as a collection of stone buildings gathered on the shore. Every day that passed cemented my certainty that here was where I belonged. Even if a black hat and

3

cloak weren't really my style. I'd borrowed the cloak from Alissa, who was a few inches taller than me, so it kept dragging on the ground unless I held it up with one hand.

We walked on, following Madame Grey's lead. The leader of the town's witches—who happened to be Alissa's grandmother as well as the head of the Meadowsweet Coven—wore a long black cloak like the rest of us, her own hat perched atop her long, curly white hair. Her voice rang across the field as she called out commands to the academy students at the front of the procession. "Left, right. That's a left, Johnson. Don't walk that way, you'll tread on someone's tail."

Sky gave a flick of his head and the hat flew off again, landing in a patch of mud. I flicked my wand. Instead of landing back on his head, the hat turned purple. *Oh, no.*

I had fewer magical disasters than I had when I'd first moved to town, but my old habits sometimes came back when I didn't pay attention. Holding my wand hand steady, I gave it another flick and the hat turned back to its normal colour. Then I darted out of line to pick it up, brushing mud off the brim with my fingers.

"Blair," said Madame Grey. "Is there a problem?"

I levitated the hat back onto Sky's head. "No, Madame Grey."

Thankfully, Sky seemed to get the message and walked into line. Just when I'd started to relax, he gave a loud, fake sneeze, and the hat went flying into the cat in front. The tabby cat turned around with a hiss of annoyance.

"Ah, sorry," I said to the familiar and its owner. "My cat is… er, allergic to fabric."

Sky gave another fake sneeze. Sometimes I wondered

if he understood every word I said, but I was more inclined to believe he pretended not to when it suited him.

The familiar's owner threw the hat back to me, and I caught it. "Thanks."

When I crouched to put it back onto Sky's head, he swiped with a claw, tearing the hat almost clean in two and snagging my wrist in the process. *Ow.*

"You okay, Blair?" Alissa's eyes widened at my bleeding wrist.

"Just wonderful." I winced. "How do you cast a repair spell again?"

And it'd all been going so well. I'd skipped to Grade Three in my magical training—passing by the skin of my teeth, thanks to the broomstick flight portion of the exam —and I'd continued with my twice-weekly lessons with Rita in my spare time after work. I'd been making strides in my progress in all areas... except for my ability to control my so-called familiar.

I picked up the torn hat and turned back to Sky, except he wasn't there. The little black cat had wandered out of the procession and down the hillside.

"Sky," I hissed. "Get back here."

He didn't turn back. Smothering a groan, I stepped out of line and hurried after him. "Sky, please. I'm not exaggerating when I say this is one of the most important events of my life."

"Miaow." Sky's tail flicked, pointing downhill towards the lake. A group of figures wearing pointed hats and cloaks walked along the path towards the town—*not* part of the procession.

They must be the visitors. My nerves spiked, and when they looked up at our procession on the hills, I froze. Hoping they couldn't see my face from a distance, I scooped up Sky, ignoring his yowl of protest, and sprinted back to my place in line.

"Blair," said Madame Grey, with exaggerated patience. "What is it now?"

"Ah—the visitors are here." I pointed over my shoulder.

"Then we'll stop for tonight." She clapped her hands. "Students, stay in line with your classmates and wait for instructions from your teachers. Everyone else, come with me to greet the newcomers."

I hovered awkwardly on the spot, not quite sure which category I fell into. I might still be a student, but I was also years older than the others at the academy. A few months of training hadn't made up for a lifetime of living in the paranormal world, but Rita, my tutor, was confident I'd catch up. In the meantime, I wouldn't have minded meeting the other coven leaders from out of town, but I'd rather they got a better first impression of me than seeing me running around the hillside after my cat.

As the group broke up, the academy's teachers summoning their students back into line to walk back to class, Madame Grey beckoned me aside. "Are you managing to keep your familiar under control?"

Sky twitched his whiskers and hid behind my legs. Madame Grey was one of the few people my cat respected, perhaps because she was the person who'd allowed me to stay in Fairy Falls to begin with. Her silver-rimmed spectacles sat on her crooked nose, magnifying her intelligent eyes. Her black hat blew sideways in the wind but somehow never fell off. Mine was attached to my cloak by a bunch of staples so the wind didn't carry it off my head, and it'd taken ages to position it so that they didn't show.

"I think he's a bit sick of the rehearsals," I admitted. "He'll be fine on the day."

"The rehearsals are for the benefit of our newest class of witches and wizards," she said. "Some of them only got their first wands in September."

My mind immediately jumped to Rebecca, the newest student at the academy—even newer than I was. She'd been put into accelerated training to catch up to her classmates, but judging by the way she stood apart from the others, she had yet to find her people. Madame Grey's sharp eyes followed my gaze to the young dark-haired witch who, personality-wise, was nothing like the rest of her family I'd met.

"You're doing a great job with her," Madame Grey added. "It's not easy being new, and she's had less life experience than you have."

"True." I'd always felt slightly out of place, even in the magical world. Having a fairy criminal for a father and a supposed thief for a mother had cemented my outsider status, to say the least. Rebecca herself had a powerful ability to influence and change others' personalities, and her mother, Mrs Dailey, had been jailed for manipulating her daughter's magic for her own gain. "I'm worried they won't look past her mother. And sister, come to that."

Blythe might not be a criminal, but she was an unpleasant individual who'd done her best to get me kicked out of town when I'd first moved to Fairy Falls. I'd taken Rebecca under my wing since I'd helped bring her mother to justice, but I couldn't protect her all the time, especially when the adult world was as full of petty bullies as the witch academy. Luckily, I'd assembled a group of friends who had my back. I could only hope that in time, Rebecca would find her own tribe who accepted her for who she was.

"Give it time," said Madame Grey. "As for your familiar, might I suggest using a spell for obedience? There are potions, too. Many witches and wizards use them all the time."

"Sky wouldn't like that." I crouched to scratch him behind the ears. "I'll make sure he behaves at the final event."

"Good," she said. "I was glad when I saw you'd signed up to take part, Blair. It's good that you're getting involved in the community more. We're happy to have you."

Even holding a muddy hat in my hand and with my cat hiding behind my ankles, my spine straightened at her implied praise. "Who are the visitors, then? Coven leaders?"

"They're not all coven leaders," she responded. "They're all the local witches who hope that the title of the region's leading witch will be passed onto them for the duration of the next year. The witches who've come here are the ones who think they're in with a chance of being picked."

I turned this information over in my mind. "The region's leading witch? How do they get picked?"

"You'll see when the event rolls around," she said. "In the meantime, I thought you might like to know that the current Head Witch was once acquainted with your mother."

My mouth fell open. "Oh. Who is she?"

"I'll introduce you," she said. "Aveline of the Hollyhock Coven has been the region's Head Witch for many years, so she's met a large number of witches and wizards, including Tanith Wildflower."

My mother. She knew my mother. Since learning of Tanith Wildflower's death, I'd been forced to conclude that nobody had really known her at all. Certainly nobody in Fairy Falls, anyway. There was a years-long gap in my mother's history from the moment she'd left Fairy Falls up until her death, and nobody in the town had seen her in the interim. Even Madame Grey hadn't been able to track down any reliable information on how my mother had come to meet my father, much less why she'd abandoned me in the foster system in the normal world before being caught by the paranormal hunters and dying before they could jail her. Which crime she'd committed to merit being chased by the most feared magical police force in the region, I could only imagine.

Not that I knew much more about my dad, except that he was alive, a fairy, and incarcerated in the Lancashire Prison for Paranormals himself. While he sent me letters from jail, he refused to tell me anything significant in case our correspondence was interrupted, including *why* he'd been locked up and whether he and my mother had committed the same crime. I wouldn't be able to see my dad until the winter solstice in two months' time, so it wouldn't hurt to talk to someone else who might have known the witch side of my family. At this point, I'd pounce on any opportunity to speak to someone who'd known her.

"Thank you," I said. "Why did they pick Fairy Falls as the location of the ceremony?"

"I volunteered the town because I thought it would improve our credibility in the eyes of the other covens," Madame Grey explained. "In any case, I also planned to make a bid for the position of Head Witch myself."

"Oh. I hope you get it." Madame Grey had faced betrayals from within her own witch council and still remained one of the strongest people I'd met. If anyone deserved the position of the leading witch in the region, it was her.

Madame Grey's sharp eyes fixed on a spot further down the hillside. "Looks like they're on the way. Since you're here, Blair, would you like to meet them now? Go and fetch Alissa, and I'll take you down to speak with the Head Witch."

My gaze followed hers, finding the group of figures from earlier had drawn closer to our dispersing procession. All appeared to be female and wore long travelling cloaks. Some also wore hats, while the leader used a cane to navigate the marshy ground.

"Oh, sure." I hastened to Alissa's side, crossing my fingers behind my back that Sky would behave. At least he wouldn't have to wear a hat for this part.

Alissa and I descended the hillside behind Madame Grey, along with our familiars.

The woman with the cane lifted it into the air, revealing it to be an elegantly carved stick which glowed with a purplish light, reflecting the wrinkles on its owner's face. She had to be at least eighty, and that cane... wasn't a cane. A halo of purple light surrounded it, and the air turned static, making the hairs on my arms stand on end. *It's a wand—but a powerful one.*

"It is a great honour to welcome the current Head Witch, Aveline Hollyhock," said Madame Grey.

I leaned closer to Alissa. "What's she carrying?"

"That's the sceptre which only the Head Witch wields," she whispered back. "They say it was created by the first coven in the region over a thousand years ago. It's so powerful that it doesn't belong to a single person, and it changes hands each Samhain. On Saturday, it'll select one witch to bear its power for the year to come."

"The sceptre chooses a person? How does that work?" I didn't know of any wands that changed owners, but the rippling currents of purple light surrounding the sceptre were unlike anything I'd ever seen in the magical world before.

The sceptre's carrier turned to me. "And what do we have here?"

"Aveline," said Madame Grey, "meet Alissa, my granddaughter, and Blair Wilkes, the newest witch to enter Fairy Falls."

"New, are you? You're a bit tall for a six-year-old."

It probably wasn't polite not to laugh at the Head Witch's jokes, so I forced a weak chuckle. "Uh, I'm twenty-five."

"I might be old, but I'm no fool, Blair Wilkes. What coven do you belong to?"

"Meadowsweet… by adoption." *For now.* My mother's coven was extinct, but now didn't seem the time to bring her up. Not with the other witches scrutinising me. Aveline wouldn't know I was related to Tanith Wildflower

11

by looking at me, considering my human appearance was technically a fairy glamour I'd been wearing all my life.

"This is not suitable weather to stand outside," Madame Grey said. "Come along, and I'll show you our coven's headquarters.

She beckoned, and the group of witches followed her. Behind the Head Witch, three witches walked in a huddle, grumbling about the cold, drizzly weather.

"The Head Witch isn't what I expected," Alissa said. "Then again, she *is* eighty-seven, and has been carrying that sceptre for years."

"So it can pick the same person each year?" I asked.

"Yes," she said. "I guess there hasn't been any competition for a while. I'm kind of surprised my grandmother is trying to claim it. She never showed any ambitions to rule over the region before—one coven is quite enough."

"Not to mention the entire town," I added. "Imagine how long the council meetings to address complaints from all the local covens would last if we brought in all the other towns, too."

"Tell me about it," said Alissa. "She must have a plan for if she wins. I wouldn't have thought she'd want to leave the council unattended for long, either, considering all the trouble we've had this year. The Head Witch often has to leave town to visit the region's other magical communities."

"I assume she does have a plan." Madame Grey knew what she was doing, I was certain of that. "She told me Aveline knew my mother."

"Really?" Alissa said. "I suppose she must have met people from all over, considering she's been Head Witch for years."

"Even career criminals." I tried to keep my tone light, but failed. Just the mention of Tanith Wildflower had brought all my worries and speculations back to the surface.

"I'm sure that's not true," said Alissa.

It sounds that way. I hated to imagine my mother might have been anything other than the loving parent she'd been denied the opportunity to be, but the hunters made no mistakes when they arrested paranormals who'd committed crimes. That my dad was locked up in the most notorious paranormal prison in the northwest of England seemed to prove what Nathan's father had claimed—namely, that both my parents had been notorious thieves. My foster parents had never met my birth family, either. Wilkes was their surname, and I still felt more of a connection to them than I did to the witch who'd seen to it that I didn't grow up in the magical world at all.

I beckoned to Sky. "We should head home before it gets dark."

"I'll fix the hat," Alissa said. "Give it here."

"Sure." I handed it over gratefully. "One more week of this left. Then you can get back to sleeping all day, okay, Sky?"

"Miaow." The small black cat was hardly visible under the darkening sky as we descended the hill towards Fairy Falls.

"I think he's being very patient for a fairy cat." Alissa waved her wand, repairing the hat, and handed it back to me. "Are you seeing Nathan tonight?"

"He's on security duty again," I said. "Making sure

nobody plans to interrupt the ceremony. Like the hunters."

"I thought they hadn't been seen in months."

"They haven't, but you never know." Even Nathan's hunter relatives hadn't come back to town since their visit over the summer. It had been Nathan's own father who'd alerted me to the fact that my mother had died—not far from here. Yet Nathan's family didn't worry me nearly as much as Inquisitor Hare, leader of the hunters, not least because he'd asked me to work for him. I'd refused, and no repercussions had come back to hit me so far, but that he knew more than I did about my family disturbed me to no end.

"I wouldn't have thought it would be their thing," Alissa said. "Celebrating Samhain, I mean. They don't seem like the partying sort."

"You're not wrong." With the exception of his younger sister, Erin, Nathan's family had disliked me from the outset and thoroughly disapproved of both me *and* Fairy Falls. It hadn't helped that Sky had shown up at my first dinner with my boyfriend's family and sat on the table, then invited a pixie into the house.

Yet despite our rocky start, Nathan and I were doing just fine, considering we only got to see one another once or twice a week. His obligations as the leader of the town's security team kept him busy, while with my own packed schedule, it was a miracle I found time to sleep, let alone hang out with my boyfriend.

Alissa and I made our way through the quiet, winding streets of the town. Sky nudged my ankle as we drew close to home. The large brick house was divided into flats, owned by Madame Grey herself, who... stood on the doorstep, along with the rest of the visiting witches. Aveline turned to face us when we approached, leaning on her walking stick.

"There you are, Blair," said Madame Grey. "Won't you and Alissa help the others get settled in?"

I blinked. "Um, settled in?"

"Didn't you know?" she said. "The potential Head Witches will be staying in your house."

2

From the shock on Alissa's face, she hadn't expected guests, either.

"Didn't you get my message?" asked Madame Grey.

Well, no. The Head Witch looked up at the house and wrinkled her nose, as though it was a run-down hovel, not one of the grandest properties in town.

"I've been at work all day," said Alissa. "I barely made it in time for the rehearsal. Where are they staying, upstairs?"

There were six witches, all cloaked and carrying suitcases. It would be hard to fit them into one room, which was probably why Madame Grey had volunteered our house to serve as accommodation. It would have been nice to be forewarned, considering Sky reacted unpredictably to strangers. He hid behind my ankles, eyeing the witches with a distrusting expression.

"They'll be staying in the empty ground-floor flat and

the upstairs one," Madame Grey said. "I think that's all for now. Do call me if you need anything."

She turned and strode away, leaving Alissa and me awkwardly standing outside with the way into the house blocked by a gaggle of suitcase-carrying witches. While it was no big secret that Madame Grey often rented out her properties to family and friends, the only neighbour we were on speaking terms with was Nina who lived upstairs. Our rent was very modest in comparison to the house's sheer size and impressiveness, and two of the flats were unoccupied. Still, I'd never seen so many strangers here before.

"Mother, put the suitcase down," said a female witch wearing a long green travelling cloak. "You'll hurt yourself."

"Don't talk to me as though I'm an infant," snapped Aveline. "I can still use a wand, you know."

She waved the sceptre, levitating her suitcase into the air. The woman who'd spoken to her, who was around Rita's age, moved aside to allow her elderly mother to pass through the doorway into the flat across the corridor from ours. The two of them had similar beaky features and long noses, though Aveline's were considerably more wrinkled, and her hair was grey rather than black. She gave the sceptre another casual flick, and the suitcase clattered to a halt in the middle of the living room.

"I do wish you wouldn't use the sceptre for that," said the green-cloaked witch.

"It's a wand like any other," Aveline grunted, shuffling into the room. As she and her daughter moved aside, three of the other witches made for the stairs, levitating their suitcases ahead of them. I crossed my fingers that they weren't throwing wild midnight raves. Sky didn't react well to having his sleep disturbed—and what if the pixie decided to pay me a visit again?

The memory of how the glitter-wielding little fairy had interrupted my dinner with Nathan's family occupied the top spot on my list of the five most humiliating experiences of my life, beating some strong competition. I was, as Alissa kindly put it, a magnet for disasters of all kinds. If I'd known all the regional hopefuls for the position of Head Witch would be staying in my house, I'd have asked Madame Grey to purchase some Blair insurance on the off-chance that the roof fell on all our heads. I had trouble enough maintaining the facade of a competent witch outside the safety of my own home, let alone with so many prestigious witches staying next door.

At least I hadn't seen the pixie in weeks. Whenever I wrote a letter to my dad and left it out at night, it had always vanished by morning, yet the pixie never showed himself in front of me. Now, I was glad of it. I doubted the witches wanted to be showered with glitter in the middle of the night.

Alissa and I entered the hallway behind the last witch, who had shoulder-length blond hair and softer features than the other new arrivals. She strode into the ground-floor flat opposite ours, halting as the Head Witch gestured around the room with the sceptre. *Isn't that a safety hazard?*

"It's rather drab, isn't it?" said Aveline. "Where is the master bedroom?"

"There isn't one, mother," said her daughter. "The house is rented by several families. That's why Blair and Alissa are here, right?"

"Exactly," I said. "We live opposite you. There are two bedrooms in this flat, right?"

"Only two?" Aveline tutted. "What a disgrace. I suppose Madame Grey wanted to put us in this dump to build character. I'm eight-seven years old and I need my comforts." She hobbled across the room, which was the exact opposite of a dump in every way.

"Um, this house is actually bigger than my grandmother's," Alissa said. "It's the best we have. You don't live in a palace, do you?"

"Do you think you're amusing, young witch?" she enquired. "No, I do not live in a palace, but I expect the basic necessities." She gave a dismissive gesture at the well-made wooden furniture, the modern kitchen appliances, and the comfy armchairs.

"Such as...?" I arched a brow.

"A fireplace, for one. These old bones get cold." She waved the sceptre and a fireplace sprang into existence in front of the armchairs.

"Where did you get that from?" Alissa asked.

"Nowhere that will miss it." Aveline gave a harsh laugh, and my dislike of her multiplied tenfold. No spell could conjure anything out of nowhere, so there was a chance the fireplace's owner would march over here and blame us for the Head Witch's thievery.

Surveying the room with satisfaction, Aveline waved the sceptre and moved the sofa directly in front of the fireplace. Then she sat down, in a manner that suggested she wouldn't get up again even if the house caught fire. "Much better. These modern houses aren't equipped for witches like me."

"The house is a hundred years old," Alissa informed her. "Is there anything we can help you with?"

"Aren't you Madame Grey's granddaughter?" said the Head Witch's daughter, eying Alissa curiously.

"Oh, we're doing introductions?" said Aveline. "This is Vanessa, my daughter and second in command. I play favourites, otherwise she'd never have got anywhere in life. Hopeless, that one."

That's nice. Vanessa grimaced and ducked her head but didn't look surprised at her mother's dismissal. I could only assume she'd built up an immunity to Aveline's barbed comments.

"I'm Alissa Grey," said Alissa.

"And you're here to put in a bid for the position of Head Witch?" said Aveline, scanning Alissa with her sharp, clever eyes.

"Oh, no," she said. "My grandmother is, so I'm sitting this one out."

"How dull," said Aveline. "Nothing wrong with a little healthy competition. It's why my daughter's here. I wouldn't have suffered to put up with her nagging otherwise."

I frowned. "You're competing against one another?"

"We would both prefer it if the sceptre remained within our coven," said Vanessa.

"That's allowed, then?" I asked.

"That's allowed?" Aveline hooted. "This one has a lot to learn. Didn't you see the Rosemary witches? All three of them are competing against one another for the prize."

"They're upstairs," said Alissa. "So it's just you two, and…?" She indicated the bedroom at the far end, into which the blond witch had disappeared.

"That's Shannon," said Aveline. "From the unfortunately-named Gooseberry Coven."

"And the sceptre will pick one of you on Samhain?" That meant they'd be staying in our house for a week.

"Yes, it will." Aveline lifted the sceptre in a wide sweep that caused her suitcase to fly across the room, almost knocking her daughter off her feet in the process.

I backed out of range. "We'll let you get on with it, then."

Alissa and I went into our own ground-floor flat. The furniture was old but sturdy, while the place was warm and inviting despite the chill outside.

"Who needs a fireplace when you have magic?" I hung up my cloak and propped my hat on the top shelf beside the front door. "I think someone's been spoiled for too long."

"That's one way of putting it." Alissa removed her cloak and hat, hanging them up beside mine. "My grandmother never spoke of Aveline in a favourable light. She must be certain this is the right decision."

"Not that it's her who's making the sacrifice." I scanned the room in search of Sky and spotted him sulking under the sofa. "Come out, Sky. I'll give you a treat."

I went to the cupboard and fetched the bag of cat treats, but Sky refused to emerge.

"He's never seen so many strangers before, has he?" Alissa stroked her own familiar, who was hiding behind a cushion. "Roald is a little nervous, too."

Her own familiar was typically friendly with everyone, but the sheer racket coming from across the corridor suggested the other witches were moving furniture around. Or conjuring up more fireplaces from other people's houses. Being the Head Witch must mean being able to get away with a lot, but I sincerely hoped the police wouldn't show up on the doorstep and pin the blame on us.

Sky reached out a paw, snatched the treat, and withdrew under the sofa again. Fairy cats could be incredibly stubborn when they wanted to be.

"They're only staying until Samhain, right?" I walked over to Sky's food bowl and left another treat there in the hopes of coaxing him out from under the sofa.

"I hope so," said Alissa. "Some might stay until the fifth of November..."

"You mean bonfire night." I returned the bag of treats to the cupboard and washed my hands in the kitchen sink. "Is that a thing in the magical world? Or was Guy Fawkes actually a wizard?"

"They say he was," she said. "Not a very good one, but the magical world does like an excuse for a celebration. Anyway, we'll just have to show up for the ceremony on Samhain. The other witches will stay out of the way the rest of the time."

"Except for the part where they're living in our house," I added. "I assume they want to keep to themselves." *I hope.*

"I doubt they'll be into wild partying, at least." She sank into the armchair, Roald climbing into her lap.

"Just as long the elves don't decide to pay another early morning visit."

"Ah." She stroked Roald. "They haven't bothered you for a while, have they?"

"I'm still recovering from August, to be honest." The

last time the elves had shown up to demand a favour from me, they'd crashed my boyfriend's dinner party in front of most of his family, and the pixie had thrown glitter all over the dining room. Not an experience I wanted to repeat in front of a bunch of prestigious witches. Or, well, ever.

There was a loud crash. Roald jumped out of Alissa's lap, and she got to her feet. "I'd better make sure they haven't broken the furniture. My grandmother would kill me."

"It's hardly your fault if they have, since the Head Witch is…" I cut myself off, seeing the door to the flat opposite ours was still open.

"It's an absolute disgrace!" said Aveline, who was on her feet once again. "This is no accommodation fit for a witch of my stature. I will not sleep in here."

Oh, great. What was her issue this time?

"What's the problem?" asked Alissa. "Should I call my grandmother?"

"Certainly *not,*" said Aveline. "Shannon took the last room."

"I sleepwalk," said the blond witch, who stood in the doorway to one of the bedrooms. "I also cast spells in my sleep, so my wand has to be kept in a different room if you don't want to wake up with no eyebrows."

"Be reasonable, mother," Vanessa told Aveline. "I don't mind sleeping on the floor to give you more space."

"I'm eighty-seven," she said. "I can't sleep in a cupboard like that."

"What's wrong with that room?" I peered over her shoulder into a room that looked almost identical to

ELLE ADAMS

mine, except with a view of the front garden rather than the back.

"I need an open window to sleep," she said.

"You can open the window." I pulled out my wand and unlocked it. "See?"

"Don't play smart with me, witchling." She jabbed the sceptre in the direction of the window. "See that? Lavender. I'm allergic. Give it a few hours and my face will puff up to the size of a melon. And I am *not* sleeping on a sofa."

"Why not conjure up something more comfortable?" Alissa said delicately.

"I'm not having people trampling through the room at all hours of the morning. I need my beauty sleep." She glared around at all of us. "Will you deny the Head Witch a suitable room?"

"I think Nina might have a free bed upstairs," Alissa said. "We can ask her. I'm sure she won't mind."

"No, I must stay on the ground floor. My hip won't stand to climb stairs."

Oh, no. I could see where this was going.

Sure enough, she turned to me next. "Does your room have a view of the garden?"

"Well, yes," I said. "But it's small and cramped, like a cupboard." And occupied by a cat, when he wasn't hiding under the sofa.

"I suppose that will have to do," she said. "Let me see it."

"It's just I have a cat." Sky could sleep anywhere, but he was in a grumpy enough mood already. "He's very territorial."

"I've dealt with a dozen familiars in my day," she said,

24

waving the sceptre as though to sweep me aside. "They can be disciplined."

Uh... I'm not sure you've ever met a fairy cat before.

Vanessa approached me, and in a lowered voice, she said, "We can compensate you. Trust me, it's best to let her have her way."

"There are herbs outside my window as well." I addressed the Head Witch. "You might be allergic to those, too."

"I'll be the judge of that." She marched across the room, forcing me to back out into the corridor or else get mowed down by the sceptre.

Vanessa followed her mother into our flat, nodding her head apologetically. Sky hissed from underneath the sofa, but the elderly witch didn't give him a second's glance. Another few steps and she stood in the entryway to my room. "Hmm. A little small, but better than the others."

"It's the same size as the other rooms." I indicated the window. "And as I said—we grow herbs for spells in the back garden."

She waved the sceptre and the window sprang open. "No lavender here. Perfect."

My heart sank. *Oh, no.*

"Are you sure you don't want to see my room?" Alissa said from behind her. "It's the same as Blair's."

"Don't you start bargaining with me, witchling, I'm too old for that nonsense." She glared at Vanessa. "Well? Are you going to fetch my suitcase or not?"

"May I please grab some of my things first?" If Aveline was a late sleeper, I'd rather have my work clothes to hand instead of having to creep past her while she was sleeping.

If *she* cast spells in her sleep, we'd all wake up as frogs the way things were going.

"Would Sky lie on her chest in her sleep out of spite?" Alissa whispered, standing in the doorway as I dragged my suitcase out from under the bed and set about piling clothes into it.

"Wouldn't put it past him," I muttered. "Roald might, too. He only stopped licking my face during the night when Sky laid claim to me."

Maybe the two cats would team up to drive the old witch out of our flat. An entertaining idea, but one that would also bring more trouble to Madame Grey and Fairy Falls as a whole. *It's only for a week,* I told myself, hauling my suitcase into the living room. The sofa was comfy enough to sleep on. *That* part didn't bother me.

"What if the pixie taps on the window in the middle of the night?" I whispered to Alissa.

"It'll be fine," she said. "Most people can't see through glamour, right?"

"Good point." Besides, Aveline scared me a lot more than any potential fairy intruder did. I crouched beside the sofa and peered at Sky's eyes, the only part of him I could see. "Sky, I'm afraid Aveline, the Head Witch, is going to be sleeping in my room. We'll camp on the sofa for the next week. It'll be fun."

I'd rate being anywhere near the Head Witch about as fun as a root canal, but it couldn't be helped.

"Miaow," Sky huffed.

I reached under the sofa to stroke him, and he swiped at my fingers. "Believe me, none of us has a choice in the matter. Play nice and I'll make it up to you."

"Who are you talking to?" Aveline stampeded back into the living room.

I straightened upright then ducked again to avoid being hit by a flying suitcase. It soared across the room and landed beside my bedroom door. "My familiar. He's wary of strangers."

"Then he's not much of a familiar, is he?" she said. "In my day, they were independent creatures. These modern familiars have grown soft."

Sky made an audible hissing noise.

"What's that?" Adeline said sharply.

"Nothing." I climbed to my feet. "Uh, is there anything I can help you with?"

She waved her sceptre in answer, and the mattress rose off my bed, tipping the covers onto the floor. "I prefer to face the window as I sleep."

Considering she held one of the most powerful magical objects in the region in her hand, I was better off not starting an argument. Instead, I backed out of the way as she rearranged my bed, scattering pillows everywhere.

"So, what can you do?" she asked. "You must have a powerful talent for Madame Grey to show an interest in you."

I grabbed some of the discarded pillows before one of us tripped over them. "I can tell whether someone's telling the truth or lying. And I can sense what type of para-normal anyone I see is, even if it isn't obvious."

I'd also blocked a vampire from reading my mind and had seen through illusion spells few other people could, but some of that was down to my fairy magic. If Madame Grey hadn't told the newcomers I was half fairy, I wasn't about to enlighten them on the subject. Even my lie-sensing ability was a combination of the mind-magic I'd inherited from my witch mother and my fairy heritage, since fairies were unable to lie.

She grunted. "I've known a few people with that sort of power. None of them turned out well."

I piled the pillows onto the armchair. "What do you mean?"

"The truth is never easy to face, Blair," she said. "And witches whose abilities enable them to control others always end up abusing that power in the end."

"Not me." It was true that other witches with similar abilities had caused me no end of difficulties since my arrival in the magical world. Blythe, my former co-worker, had used her mind-reading powers to humiliate me, while her mother had used a similar skill to attempt to unseat Madame Grey from her position as leader of the town's council. But that didn't mean I'd ever use my own abilities in the same way.

Aveline gave another grunt. "Time will tell. Do unpack my suitcase for me, Blair, will you?"

———

I couldn't sleep. Not because the sofa was uncomfortable, but because Sky had decided the next best thing to sleeping on my bed was to sprawl across my chest. Whenever I tried to move to a more comfortable position, he Sky twitched and flailed in his sleep and speared me with his claws. My back and neck ached, while the sound of Aveline snoring drifted through my open bedroom door, accompanied by the patter of rain on the windowsill.

Aveline had spent the entire evening giving orders to

Vanessa and complaining at full volume. She'd resisted all my attempts to steer the conversation onto the topic of my mother, not out of deliberate avoidance of the subject but because she preferred to dictate the conversation and everyone else to shut up and listen to her. By now, I had a headache and a strong desire to find somewhere else to sleep. Like a tent on the lawn, for instance.

Sky jerked awake, swatting at something above my head. I winced when his claws dug into my skin through my pyjamas and sat up, looking for the intruder. A small winged shape flitted about overhead—the pixie.

I made shooing motions with my hand, but Sky kept batting at the pixie with his paws. I lifted him off me and stood, stretching my aching limbs. Tilting my head, I mouthed at the pixie, *please don't wake anyone up.* At least he hadn't come in via Aveline's room. But I'd left my slippers under my bed, and I didn't dare risk waking her.

I grabbed my shoes instead, following the pixie outside the flat. I tried to make as little noise as possible, but Aveline's resonant snoring followed me all the way down the corridor. She'd also left the back window open, so I moved deeper into the garden to speak to the pixie without waking her. When tall rows of flowering plants blocked the house from view, I stopped, shivering.

"What are you here for?" I whispered to the pixie. "It might have escaped your attention, but we have visitors. Important ones."

The pixie dropped a scrap of paper onto my head in answer. I unfolded the note to read my dad's latest message.

Samhain is the one day of the year when the barriers between worlds are the thinnest. They say you can see fairies on

29

that night. They also say the dead often come back to talk to the living.

I read the note again, then once more. What was he implying? That I'd be able to see the fairies? Or speak to the dead…

Like my mother?

I folded the note in my hand. "Does he mean I can talk to my mum? Or is he implying more fairies are coming?"

The pixie flew in a circle, then vanished.

"Hey!" I moved, then realised the sound of snoring from the house had quietened. *Uh-oh.*

Bracing myself, I walked back towards the house. Sure enough, Aveline watched me through my bedroom window, a scowl on her face.

"What in the goddess's name are you doing?" she said loudly.

"Uh, taking a midnight walk to gather herbs." I grabbed a few stems at random. "Don't worry, I'm coming back inside now."

I entered the house through the back door, regretting my midnight jaunt already. As I tiptoed through the dark corridor, a furious shout came from inside my flat. So much for not waking everyone.

I pushed open the door and found Aveline standing in the centre of the room, an expression of livid fury on her face.

"It's gone," she announced.

"What's gone?" I let the door close behind me, wishing I'd just stayed put. I should have known she'd be a light sleeper.

Alissa's bedroom door opened, and she walked out, yawning. "What is it?"

"The sceptre's missing," said Aveline.

What?

"It is?" I said. "Are you sure it didn't roll under the bed?"

"Of course not," she snapped. "It was right there. But now it's gone."

Oh, no. Tired though I was, I'd have to find the sceptre if we wanted to get any peace. I walked into my bedroom to look around. She'd moved all my furniture, but the sceptre wasn't exactly difficult to spot. I crouched to look under the bed. Nothing. Not in the wardrobe either.

It seemed she was right. Someone had broken into our flat… and stolen the sceptre.

3

A veline hobbled around with such ferocity, I braced myself in case she tripped and hurt herself. "Where is it?"

"Where did you leave it last night?" I gave the room another scan, making a mental list of all the possible places it could have disappeared to. I was certain I'd seen her take it into my bedroom when she'd retired to bed, but I searched the bathroom, then the kitchen.

Alissa came out of her own room. "It's not in here."

"Search the living room, then," Aveline snapped. "I'm not going back to bed until we find it."

While she herded Alissa into the living room, I re-entered my bedroom and searched under the bed once again. Then I checked in the wardrobe, in the drawers, under the mattress. I even checked outside the open window, and behind the curtains. No sign of it.

"Are you positive you didn't move it during the night?" I exited the room, finding Alissa dutifully searching under the armchairs.

"What do you take me for? I was asleep until someone woke me up by wandering around in the garden."

I wasn't even near the house. But she'd been snoring right up until I'd left, so unless the thief had sneaked in while I'd still been awake, there was only one time they could have done it: while I'd been outside.

Oh, no. I'd left the flat door unlocked. The house was in the safest part of the neighbourhood and with a fairy cat on guard duty, I'd become accustomed to leaving the flat door open whenever I went outside to see the pixie during the night. Yet the back door had been closed and the front door locked.

So… had someone *inside* the building stolen the sceptre?

Aveline reached into the pocket of her flowery dressing gown and withdrew a long, thin wand, giving it a wave. The sofa lifted into the air, rousing Sky with a yowl of dismay. The bookshelves shook themselves, sending books toppling onto the floor.

"Hey—what're you doing?" I stumbled backwards as the carpet yanked itself out from under my feet, and an armchair skidded into my kneecaps.

"What else? Turning the place upside-down."

I scooped Sky up in my arms and he clawed at my face, drawing blood. Wincing, I backed away from the levitating armchairs into the doorway. "Can't you search when we're outside?"

In answer, she tipped my suitcase upside-down, scattering my clothes all over the floor. Sky jumped out of my arms and ran, hiding underneath them. Great. Now my work clothes were covered in cat hair.

"Head Witch," said Alissa pleadingly. "You're knocking over my things—"

"Don't you dare order me around, you young whippersnapper," she said. "That sceptre is worth more than your lives."

"Mother!" Vanessa shouted from the corridor outside. "What are you doing?"

I opened the flat door to let her in. "The sceptre's missing, so she's turning the place upside-down —literally."

Vanessa entered and tripped over the rumpled carpet, grabbing the doorway for balance. "Mother, please stop. We're guests here!"

Aveline whirled on her daughter. "Someone stole the sceptre from beside me while I slept."

"I heard voices outside," said Vanessa hesitantly.

"Ah, that was me," I said. "I didn't see anyone else out there, though."

"Then who were you talking to?" Aveline's eyes narrowed. "Your accomplice in crime, perhaps?"

"Of course not," I said, insulted. "You'd have heard me if I'd come into your room. I'm guessing the thief sneaked in while I was outside, but the front door was locked, and I didn't see anyone around the back."

"So the thief came from in the house, did they?" she said. "I should have known one of the Rosemary witches would try an underhanded trick like that."

"Mother!" said Vanessa. "Please don't make unfounded accusations."

"The door was locked, she says," Aveline said.

"The thief could have used an unlocking charm," Alissa

put in. "Unless you're certain the other witches might have had reason to steal it?"

"It's no big secret that they all want my position," said Aveline. "They've been doing nothing but talking about unseating me for weeks. I won't have any of it."

"What's going on?" Nina walked downstairs, wearing a bright pink dressing gown. Her strawberry blond hair stuck out at all angles, but she looked as though she'd had a more restful night than I had.

"There was a break-in," Aveline informed her. "Someone saw fit to steal the sceptre. Unless you had designs on it yourself? Thought you'd steal a bit of power, did you?"

"No." Nina looked alarmed. "I don't even know what the sceptre does. I didn't know you had it in the flat, either." *True.* Not that I thought Nina would have taken it. She didn't have a reason to. The other Head Witch-wannabes, on the other hand...

"She's telling the truth," I said.

"And you're the expert, are you?" said Aveline.

"Mother!" said Vanessa. "Blair's trying to help."

"Also, she really can tell if people are lying," Alissa added. "If the thief is in the building, it should be easy to prove who they are."

"Is that so?" She peered at me. "And can anyone tell when *you're* lying? Convenient."

"I have no idea what you're talking about," I said irritably. I hadn't slept, our flat was a tip and I had another week of this cranky old witch to endure without losing my mind. Poor Sky let out a meow of despair from underneath my clothes.

"Did your familiar take it?" asked Aveline.

"Sky wouldn't know how to use it." But he *had* been in the room when the thief had come in. Had he seen the intruder?

I walked over to the pile of clothes. "Sky, did you see anyone come into the flat?"

"Miaow."

"What does he mean?" asked Aveline. "Can you understand him?"

I shook my head. "He can understand everything we say, but it doesn't go both ways."

Yet he'd been in the flat during the break-in, and unless they came through the window, the thief must have walked through the living room to get in. Right?

"Then we'll make him talk." Aveline pulled out her wand and gave it a wave. Sky floated upwards, dislodging clothes in the process. His claws lashed out, shredding everything they could reach.

"Hey!" I hurried over to him, but he flew higher into the air. "Stop that."

"Cat got your tongue?" Aveline looked up at Sky. "Bit small for a familiar, isn't he?"

Sky made a faint growling noise. Uh-oh. The last thing I needed was for Sky to transform into a giant monster in front of the Head Witch. "Sky, calm down. She doesn't mean it."

Aveline made a derisive snorting noise. "Do you normally speak to your familiar like that? No wonder he has no respect."

"Mother!" said Vanessa, hurrying to her side. "Blair, I'm sorry—Mother, please put him down."

"MIAOW." Sky let out a growl as he landed in my arms

in a flurry of claws. He leapt to the floor, then sprinted from the room in a streak of black fur.

"Ah—Sky, come back!" The last time Sky had vanished, he'd taken days to return. Admittedly, if I were him, I wouldn't want to come back until Aveline had departed, but if he'd seen who'd broken into the flat and there were no other witnesses, finding the thief would be a lot harder. *Thanks for that, Aveline.*

Aveline huffed. "They don't make familiars like they used to, do they? Right, Vanessa, we're going to search this whole sorry dump of a house."

The instant they left our flat, Alissa and I got to work returning the furniture to where it belonged. I won ten minutes in the bathroom to take a quick shower and change into my work clothes. They were covered in cat hair, but that was nothing new. *Why did she have to insult Sky?* He might not be a typical witch familiar, but that didn't make him disloyal. Or disrespectful. Aveline hadn't done a thing to deserve anyone's respect, besides.

If Sky thought we were in danger from whoever had broken into the flat, he'd find a way to tell me. For now, I'd figure out how to make it up to him after the week was over. Maybe I'd buy him a small mountain of bubble wrap to destroy.

I left the bathroom and went into the living room to find Nina and Alissa, the former still wearing her pink dressing gown.

"She turned my flat upside-down, too," said Nina. "How has she stayed head of the region's witches for so long without someone ousting her?"

"Better keep it down," Alissa added. "I'm so glad I'm

working from midday until midnight. I'll be able to avoid her."

"I don't like to imagine what she'll do to the place while we're at work, though," I said. "And how did the thief break in? I was outside for ten minutes, if that, and I was wide awake before then. I don't know how you slept through her snoring."

"Earplug charm," she said. "I'll teach you that one."

"If I want to get any sleep all week, I'll need it." I sank onto the sofa. "Have we definitely checked every corner?"

A crash came from overhead, followed by a scraping noise that sounded like a bed being dragged across a hardwood floor.

"I hope so," Nina said morosely. "Maybe if I offer her a free haircut, she'll leave my flat alone."

"You're out at work all day?" Nina worked at the local hairdresser's, specialising in giving fancy haircuts to local witches and wizards. Given the tangled state of the Head Witch's grey curly hair—which she'd left all over the inside of the shower—I doubted she particularly cared about fancy hairdos.

"Yes, luckily," she said. "I swear there should have been a clause in our tenancy agreement about this sort of thing. *Watch out for Head Witches.* Bring earplugs and a shedload of patience."

"She's impossible," I agreed. "Maybe one of the other witches did steal the sceptre, but you'd think they'd have waited until after the ceremony. It makes no sense to steal it beforehand, does it?"

"Good point," said Alissa. "Either they didn't expect to be chosen, or they needed it now. Who knows why, though?"

"Do either of you know what the sceptre actually does?" I asked. "Because all I know is that it's like a wand, but more powerful."

"Haven't a clue." Nina winced at another crashing noise. "Most people don't, I imagine. The sceptre's supposed to keep the balance between the covens. That's what my mum said, anyway."

"Balance?" Another crash shook the whole room, and I lunged to catch my coffee mug before it fell off the table. "She didn't have any trouble climbing the stairs this time around."

"Oh, she got her daughter to levitate her," said Alissa. "I should probably make sure she doesn't fall on the way down. It's bad enough that the sceptre's missing—we don't need to lose its owner, too."

"Even if she's completely bonkers." The thief had some serious nerve. "I'm going to see if the others escaped her rampage."

I got to my feet and headed for the flat opposite ours. Only Shannon was left, occupying the sofa in front of the stolen fireplace.

"Aren't you going to help Aveline stop her from turning everyone's rooms inside out?" I asked her.

"Not until she finds it," said Shannon. "Aveline has been Head Witch for decades. She won't give up until that sceptre is back in her hands. If one of you stole it, it's best to own up."

"None of us did," I said. "We don't even know what the sceptre can do."

"Her poor daughter," said Shannon. "I'd accuse her of wanting it for herself, but she knows better than to cross her old mother."

"She wanted the sceptre?" I asked, surprised. Maybe I shouldn't have been, since Aveline had mentioned that her daughter had come with her because she'd hoped to be chosen as Head Witch if her mother wasn't.

"She wants the title of Head Witch," Shannon corrected. "Word has it she's been waiting for years, but Aveline has clung onto the title every single year. If I were her, I'd be desperate, too."

"Vanessa's been waiting to take her mother's place?" asked Alissa. "That doesn't give her good reason to steal the sceptre from her mother's room a week before Samhain. She'd know she was disqualifying herself from ever being chosen if she was caught."

"No, I suppose it doesn't," said Shannon. "If anything, it's a sign that someone else should have been put in charge long ago. If we didn't have to follow this ridiculous farce of carting the sceptre around, then it would never have gone missing."

"Why do you have to do it, then?" I asked.

"Tradition," she said. "The sceptre is more powerful on Samhain, so the ceremony can only take place in certain locations. When the veil is thin, the sceptre can even assist in parting it."

"Parting... the veil?" My heart stuttered. "You mean, like... death?"

"Of course," said Shannon. "Have you never experienced Samhain in a witches' community before?"

Well... no. But if the *sceptre* was needed for me to contact the dead, then as long as it was missing, I could say goodbye to the possibility of ever seeing my mother. And I'd bet Aveline wouldn't be open to discussing her history with Tanith Wildflower at all if she thought me a thief. I had to try to find the real culprit if I wanted her cooperation.

"Did you hear anyone come into the house?" I asked Shannon.

"No. I sleep like the dead. Woke up pretty quickly when she started yelling, though."

True. So she wasn't the thief. That left the three witches upstairs, Vanessa… and Aveline herself.

Loud footsteps came from above. Then the Head Witch ordered, "Go on, levitate me down."

Vanessa's long-suffering voice said, "Please keep still this time."

"I hope she drops her," muttered Shannon. "I feel awful for you two, having to put up with her. She'll make our lives a misery until that sceptre shows up, make no mistake. I'm surprised she let someone steal it from right under her nose to begin with."

Aveline sailed downstairs, landed in the hall, and hobbled into the room. "What're you all meeting in here for, then? Having a good laugh at my expense?"

"Don't be ridiculous, mother," said Vanessa from behind her. "You turfed them out of their rooms."

"The sceptre," she said, "was *stolen.* A crime like that is worth more than a life sentence. And without it, the region's magic will weaken until we're vulnerable to threats from all angles."

My phone buzzed. A message from Nathan: *How's it going?*

I'd texted him the details of Aveline's ridiculous demands last night, since I couldn't express them verbally.

Not great. Talk later?

Come to the Troll's Tavern tonight. I'll pick you up after work. x

Sure thing. x

Sorted. One thing to look forward to among a pile of horrors.

Aveline tapped her foot on the floor. "Who are you talking to? Not speaking with your partner-in-crime who helped you steal the sceptre, are you?"

"No." I looked up from the phone. "Trust me, if I was going to steal it, I'd have handed it back to you by now."

Nothing, not even a powerful object which might enable me to talk to my dead mother, was worth this much hassle.

Aveline scowled as though sensing my thoughts. I put my phone away and made for the door. "I have to go to work. If you have any leads on the thief, let me know when I'm back."

"I have to go to work, too," said Alissa, whose shift didn't start for another two hours. "I'll be back at midnight."

Aveline tutted. "Midnight? Where do you work?"

"The hospital," said Alissa.

"Ah, yes, healing magic," said Aveline. "That'll be why you're not running for the position of Head Witch. You'd rather play it safe."

"Actually, I like my job," Alissa said. "I find I get to meet much more pleasant people than I would as a coven leader."

I held back a grin. Like her, I'd much rather deal with drunken elves and mischief-causing old seers than spend another minute in Aveline's company.

"And you, Blair?" she said. "Where do you work? I

imagine being able to sense lies has proven advantageous for your employment in the magical world, otherwise it's not worth having."

"I work for Eldritch & Co," I said. "It's a magical recruitment firm."

She sniffed. "Maybe not, then. What a waste."

Knowing her, she'd have made a derisive comment even if I'd said I saved orphans for a living. "What do you think I should be doing with my talent, then?"

"Putting it to use against the forces of evil," she said. "Your police force has a shoddy record, from what I've heard."

"I have helped the police before." I approached the door, having had about enough. "But I prefer to keep a low profile."

Not that I'd ever been successful at it. By the day's end, the entire town would know the sceptre had been stolen from my *bedroom*. As for fighting the forces of evil, the cantankerous Head Witch was more than enough to deal with at the moment.

"See you later." Alissa waved goodbye to the others with a false smile fixed on her face, and the two of us left the flat.

"Are you going out with Nathan after work?" asked Alissa.

"Yes," I said. "I didn't want to mention him in front of Aveline in case she tries to chase him off like she did to Sky."

I looked under every bush in the front garden for Sky, but found no sign of him.

"He's probably asleep in the back garden," said Alissa.

43

"Sky has the right idea. If I had anywhere else to go, I would. Why not go to Nathan's?"

"He promised to rescue me from Aveline after work, but knowing my luck, he'll get called out on the night shift again." I'd all but ruled out having any chance to spend longer than a couple of hours with him this week. Especially with a thief on the loose. "Or he'll get assigned to guard the house in case someone else comes in to rob us."

"Fair point," she said. "I'm going to talk to my grandmother and see if I can't persuade her to make other arrangements for Aveline."

"Haven't you told her about the missing sceptre?" I asked.

"I have. No reply yet." She pulled her phone out of her pocket. "Madame Grey will probably want to search the house in person. Nothing gets past her."

"The thief got past the rest of us," I reminded her. "I swear, I didn't see or hear another person when I went outside. Then again, the Head Witch was snoring like a jackhammer. There could have been a live jazz band playing upstairs and I wouldn't have heard."

"The pixie got in, though."

"He's a fairy." When my phone buzzed again, I sent Nathan a quick text explaining the sceptre's theft. Maybe I should have asked him to guard the house last night, but you'd think any thief would think twice before robbing a house full of the most powerful witches in the region. "And he'd have no reason to steal a sceptre."

"Did he bring a message from your dad?" she asked.

"Yep," I said. "According to my dad, the walls between

worlds are thin around this time of year, so it's easier to talk to fairies. And ghosts."

"Whoa, Blair. Does he mean there might be other fairies who might want to meet you?"

"I don't know, but I hope they don't invite themselves into our house, too." I turned down the road that led to my workplace and eventually, the lake. "The Head Witch would turn me into a grapefruit."

"I'd pay to see her face if they did," said Alissa. "She seems to get a kick out of being unpleasant. I never thought I'd say this, but I'd rather deal with that drunken elf for an extra two hours than spend them at home."

I grimaced. "Yeah, I would, too. I guess we'll have to find creative reasons to stay away from the house every day until Samhain."

Or until we found the sceptre. Whichever came first. The theft aside, I never should have pinned any hopes on learning the truth about my mother from Aveline. Considering how the Head Witch spoke about the living, I was better off not knowing what she thought of the dead.

4

I'd almost reached the office when I heard someone calling my name. I turned around to see my boss, Veronica Eldritch, approaching with her long-legged stride. She was tall and willowy with sleek, silvery hair grown past her shoulders. "You're early this morning."

"Ah, we had visitors staying in our house last night," I said, unsure whether she'd heard about the theft yet. Considering Madame Grey had yet to respond, I'd guess not, and I doubted she'd want me to spread word around town.

"Oh, that Aveline Hollyhock," said Veronica. "I heard she's held onto the position of Head Witch with a steel grip for years, but she's starting to slip. I hope security is tight at the Samhain ceremony."

So do I, especially if the sceptre doesn't show up by then. "You aren't going?"

"I never did have much patience for ceremonies." She strode ahead of me through the automatic doors into

Dritch & Co's office. "That Head Witch position is a prime example of a tradition which should be left in the past."

I blinked, somewhat surprised. Though maybe I shouldn't have been. Veronica Eldritch and her company were modern, through and through, down to the computers fitted with paranormal technology and her personal office which redecorated itself according to her mood. I couldn't picture her striding around a muddy field waving a sceptre around.

"I'm a bit lost on what the title actually represents," I admitted. "Of Head Witch, I mean."

"Stability," she said. "The town's reputation doubtless needs it. I, however, have no interest whatsoever."

We entered the reception area, where Callie the blond werewolf sat behind the front desk. She waved at me as I walked past, reaching the door which led into the main office. Bethan, the boss's daughter, already sat at her desk. She and her mother were both tall and lean, but she had black hair where her mother's was white.

"Hi, Blair," she said. "You have a sock sticking out of your shirt, did you know?"

Oops. Either Veronica hadn't looked closely, or she thought I was trying to make a fashion statement. Feeling my face heat, I extracted the sock and slipped it into my bag. "My cat messed up my clothes this morning. We have a bunch of local coven representatives staying in our house and I had to give up my room, so I'm not completely with it today."

"Are you ever?" said Lizzie, the dark-skinned witch who sat at the desk opposite mine. She wore her hair in barrettes today.

47

"Very funny." I sat down in my swivel chair, finding a mug on my desk. "Who made me coffee?"

"I did." Rob stuck his blond head over the computer beside Lizzie's. "Morning, Blair."

I picked up the mug. "You're a lifesaver."

When Callie's cousin had first applied to work at the office, I'd been less than thrilled, since his uncle wasn't my biggest fan, but Rob was a dream employee. He arrived to work two hours early to tidy the place almost every day and had a gift for calming down the most agitated clients. As a result, it was hard to dislike the guy. I sat down and took a huge sip of coffee, wincing as it took a layer of skin off the roof of my mouth.

"I should have warned you it's hot," he said. "Rough night?"

"An elderly witch who snores is sleeping in my room." I put down the mug and turned to today's list of tasks.

"Not Aveline Hollyhock?" said Bethan, her brows rising. "I heard Madame Grey made you play host to the potential Head Witches, but I didn't know you had to give up your room."

"Aveline can't climb stairs and the other rooms had the wrong plants outside the window." I stifled a yawn. "She strong-armed me into giving her my room, rearranged my furniture, and chased off my cat."

"I'd have set my familiar on her if she'd done it to me," said Lizzie.

"Me, too," Bethan said. "Didn't Madame Grey consult you first?"

"She doesn't know I gave up my room," I said. "I'll be giving her an earful the next time I see her, believe me."

Somewhat difficult, considering we now had a thief to find as well as a half-dozen witches to accommodate.

Bethan's phone buzzed, and she pulled it out. "Huh. Is it true that the sceptre was stolen?"

So much for keeping it quiet. "Did Alissa tell you? I wasn't sure I was allowed to tell anyone yet."

Of course, Aveline was probably shouting from the rooftops. If the sceptre's absence continued, everyone on this side of the lake would be aware of it by the end of the morning.

"It was taken from your room?" said Bethan. "Do you have any idea who might have done it?"

I shook my head. "Either one of the other potential Head Witches, or someone with really good timing. Or bad, depending on how you look at it."

"What do you mean?" asked Rob.

"I wasn't inside the house when it happened," I explained. "I went for a walk to get away from Aveline's snoring. I was barely gone ten minutes and the thief would have had to move fast to get through the back door without me seeing them. The front door was locked. Anyway, the Head Witch is blaming everyone else in the house, since they were all hoping to claim the sceptre on Samhain."

The office door opened, and Veronica sailed in. "Are you working?"

Bethan looked up. "I just heard the sceptre was stolen."

"Oh, that," she said. "Let the council sort out their squabbles in their own time."

Her flippancy surprised me given her remarks about security at the ceremony, but then again, the sceptre didn't seem to mean much to anyone except for the Head

ELLE ADAMS

Witch hopefuls. Which suggested one of them must have stolen it, but I hadn't had the chance to use my lie-sensing powers on all the others yet. If the sceptre was hidden elsewhere in the house, Aveline's insistence on searching every inch of the place would surely turn it out soon enough. Given that none of the visitors was familiar with the town layout, where else could they have hidden the sceptre in the short time it had taken Aveline to notice it was missing?

After the eventful start I'd had to the day, dealing with clients was a welcome relief, and left me little time to ponder how to survive the rest of the week with Aveline occupying my room. Maybe finding the sceptre would land me in her good books, but I doubted it.

I looked up from my work to find Rob watching me across the desk. "Blair, this is going to sound kind of weird, but I have an easy way to tell if anyone broke into your flat or not. Werewolves have a very strong sense of smell. We don't normally get involved in these sorts of situations, but considering how important that sceptre is, I'd be happy to come and sniff around."

"Not sure the Head Witch wants any more visitors," I said. "Madame Grey is searching the place at the moment. Thanks for the offer, though."

I'd forgotten about werewolves' powerful sense of smell, but a lot of people had been in that room since Aveline had turned the place inside-out. Including Aveline herself. For all I knew, she'd faked the whole thing for attention, or so she wouldn't have to give the sceptre up at the ceremony on Samhain.

"Anytime," said Rob. "Just give me a shout if you'd like me to look around for trouble."

"I might take you up on that, if Madame Grey doesn't find anything." If not to find the sceptre, then to find my missing familiar. Sky might be able to set the record straight if he really had witnessed the break-in, but given his traumatic experience at the Head Witch's hands, I'd be lucky if he showed up before the Samhain ceremony.

Perhaps he'd gone back to the bookshop where I'd first found him. Or Vincent's place, since the two had been friends before Sky had adopted me. Not only that, Vincent had mind-reading powers, and they extended to being able to communicate with Sky—on some level, at least.

Might he be able to use that ability to find out if Sky had seen the sceptre's thief?

As soon as the workday finished, I set out for the vampires' main headquarters. The uphill walk was refreshing and helped revive me a little. Above, the cloudy sky promised rain, and the odds of us conducting the Samhain ceremony in the drizzle were depressingly high. *Just as long as I'm not also without a familiar. Hat or no hat.*

Grand houses stood at intervals on either side of me, surrounded by high fences, indicating that I was heading the right way. Soon enough, I reached the sooty-coloured building that squatted next to the local cemetery like a grumpy shadow. While you might think the vampires had picked the location for the novelty value, they also ran the town's funeral home. Just in case any of the dead bodies got up and started walking—which was an occupational hazard of living in a magical town.

I halted outside the door and knocked, hoping Vincent was in. I didn't quite understand vampires' sleeping habits, but they were rumoured to sleep at dawn and wander around at night. I also wasn't sure who actually lived here, considering the lack of wards on the doors, but perhaps the vampires expected nobody to dare break into a building filled with coffins inhabited by dozing predators.

The door opened with a faint creak and Madame Grey's youngest granddaughter, Sammi, walked out. "Oh," she said. "Hi, Blair."

"Hey, Sammi." I looked past her to see Vincent approach the door, his hair slicked back and his face waxwork-pale, like a walking statue dressed in a black suit and tie.

"It's been a pleasure talking to you, Miss Grey," Vincent said. "Blair, how may I help you today?"

I glanced over my shoulder as Sammi walked away. "What was she doing here?"

"She came to speak with me about her school history project," Vincent said. "I humoured her. What can I help you with?"

"My cat," I said. "He ran away from my flat earlier, as you probably read from my mind as soon as I looked at you."

Vampires' mind-reading powers were as potent as my lie-sensing abilities, which told me his claim that Sammi had come here for help with a school project was the truth, at least. I wondered if her grandmother knew she was hanging out with vampires after school.

"Your cat," he said. "No, I haven't seen him. Why did he run away from you this time?"

Judging by the way he'd carefully dodged my statement about his mind-reading, I surmised that I'd accidentally blocked his thought-sensing power again. It happened sometimes, but I had no idea how to control it. Yet another quirk I'd picked up from my mother.

"You might have heard the hopefuls for the position of Head Witch are in town," I began. "Well, they're staying in my house, and Aveline Hollyhock and Sky didn't exactly hit it off."

"Ah," he said. "Yes, I heard about the theft, too. I rather think the timing couldn't be worse, for the town and for the council."

At least he already knows. If the thief wasn't found before Samhain, it would reflect badly both on Madame Grey and on Fairy Falls as a whole. And on me, if Aveline persisted in flinging the blame in my direction.

"Has Sky sent any images to you today?" I asked. "I mean, through your psychic link or whatever it is?"

"No," he said. "Why?"

"He might have been the only witness to whoever stole the sceptre," I admitted. "They slipped in and out of my flat while I was outside, and he was the only person in the living room. Aveline was asleep, and so were Alissa and her familiar."

He watched me unblinkingly, his expression giving nothing away. The vampire was notoriously stingy when it came to helping others out, and anything that didn't directly involve himself and his fellow vampires was generally of little interest to him. Being eight hundred years old meant picking his battles carefully. Past experience told me not to get my hopes up, and sure enough, he shook his head.

"I will keep an eye out for that feline of yours," he said. "In the meantime, I'd suggest you employ that useful talent of yours."

He means questioning the other witches using my power. I did plan to, and they'd be more likely to talk to me than the mind-reading vampire—marginally, anyway. "If you see Sky, will you let me know? I have to make sure Aveline hasn't destroyed my room while I've been at work."

I also needed to change before my date with Nathan, but given the sock incident earlier, I'd be lucky to remember to put clean shoes on. Then again, Nathan often showed up for our dates with mud on his clothes from patrolling the town's borders on security duty. We were still in the deliriously happy Honeymoon phase of our relationship where it didn't matter if we both arrived to our dates covered in swamp water.

"Then you had better leave." Vincent smiled, with a flash of fang. "It's always a pleasure seeing you, Blair."

Lie. He knew I could sense it, but he let me hear it anyway. *Vampires.* Shaking my head, I turned and made my way back downhill towards home.

I found Vanessa sitting on the doorstep of our house. She sprang to her feet when she spotted me.

"What are you doing out here?" I glanced at the window, but the curtains were drawn.

Vanessa stepped aside to let me into the house. "My own *mother* thinks I stole the sceptre. She threw me out."

"And did you?" I asked.

Her expression turned to blank shock. "Why—no, not at all."

True. "Sorry, I've had a long day," I said. "I can also tell if someone's lying or not, so I figured I'd get it over with. Are the others in?"

"The Rosemary witches?" A flash of some unidentifiable emotion appeared in her eyes. "Yes, they are. So... if you ask every person in the house if they stole the sceptre, you'd know if they lied?"

"Yeah, I would," I said. "Within reason. I mean, if the thief came from outside the house, I'd need more clues before figuring out who to pursue. Questioning everyone in town is too time-consuming."

Not to mention the thief might not even be *from* Fairy Falls, if any of the other witches had brought outside help. That was the only possible reason I could think of for the sceptre not turning up in the house after the havoc Aveline had wreaked on it.

"I suppose the circumstances seem to point to the culprit being among us guests," she mused. "However, my mother was very thorough in her search of the house."

"I'm amazed it's still standing," I said. "Has my cat come back?"

"No." Vanessa shifted from one foot to the other. "Blair, I have to apologise for my mother's actions. She's normally respectful of other witches' familiars."

"She doesn't respect you, does she?" I clamped my mouth shut before I made a more unwise statement. "I mean, what made her label you as the culprit? Because you want the sceptre yourself?"

"It's not the sceptre I wanted," said Vanessa. "It's the position of Head Witch, which has to be earned. Stealing the sceptre for its own sake would defeat the purpose. I wanted the position of Head Witch to stay within our coven, whether I was chosen or not."

True. "So that's why you came here?"

"Yes." She drew herself upright. "I did."

"I'll talk to the others, including the Head Witch, but I

can't promise she'll listen." I suspected Aveline's daughter was the only person who came close to getting some sense out of the old witch—and not by much.

Inside the house, I heard voices behind my flat door. I opened it to find Aveline playing some kind of card game with the three Rosemary witches from upstairs. The oldest of the three had magenta hair and wore floral clothes bright enough to require sunglasses to look at. The two other witches appeared to be identical twins. While their hair was chestnut brown, one of them wore yellow and the other wore red, in equally bright shades.

"Oh, it's you, Blair," said Aveline.

"Yes, it is." *Since I live here.* "What are you four doing?"

"Playing Scrabble," said the pink-haired witch. "I'm winning."

"That's because you always cheat, mother," said the twin on her right-hand side, who wore yellow.

I turned to the Head Witch. "I take it the thief is still at large?"

Aveline ignored me, focusing her attention on the game.

The pink-haired witch spoke instead. "I don't believe we've been introduced yet. I'm Grace Rosemary. These are my daughters, Patience and Charity."

"Hi." I waved awkwardly. "I'm Blair. As you probably know by now."

The two witches muttered hellos.

"Very nice house you have here," added Grace.

It was even nicer before a certain someone rearranged it. "Thanks. So have none of you seen any signs of the thief?"

"No," said the pink-haired witch. "Devilish quick, weren't they? I'm impressed."

"Aren't you the one who was sleeping in here when the thief sneaked in?" asked the twin on the right, who wore red.

"No, I was outside." And I thoroughly regretted that stroll, considering how much of a waste of time it'd been. "Have you seen the sceptre today?"

A chorus of 'no's followed. My lie-sensing power didn't go off, which ought to prove they weren't responsible for the theft. But then, who might it be? The only people not in the room were Shannon and Vanessa.

"We didn't take it," Grace said. "I'd very much like to see who did, though."

True. I gave a nod, and the witch in red—Charity—turned in my direction. "I heard you can sense lies."

"I can." I should have known at least one of them would have worked it out. I hadn't exactly been subtle with my questions. "Has Madame Grey been here?"

"She came and went." Aveline waved a hand. "Didn't find anything, of course. Whoever has that sceptre knew where to hide it."

I glanced over my shoulder, seeing Vanessa's miserable profile still hunched outside the door. "I used my lie-sensing power on your daughter, too. She didn't steal the sceptre. She wants to earn the position of Head Witch the right way."

"I know," said Aveline. "She's depressingly moral."

"So why did you kick her out?" I edged past her to the corner where I'd stored my suitcase.

"We need a security guard," she said.

"You could have used my cat," I said. "Have either of you seen him?"

"No," she said. "Oh, don't look so disgusted. My

daughter's a grown woman who can make her own choices."

Not if they're forced on her. I held my tongue and opened my suitcase, digging through cat-hair-covered outfits in the hope of finding something clean to wear for my date with Nathan.

"Nice underwear," said Grace from behind me.

I flushed and dropped the pile of clothes I'd picked up. "I normally keep my clothes in my room, but—"

"But you generously donated it to Aveline here." She gave a yellow-toothed grin as though she'd told a hilarious joke. "Pink is not your colour."

"I'll take that under advisement." Face flaming, I headed into the bathroom. Dumping my clothes in a heap, I frowned at the walls, which were splattered with neon pink. "What happened in here?"

"Oh, I dyed my hair in your bathroom," said Grace. "Aveline said I could."

You might know it. "Aveline doesn't live here."

"For this week, I do," said the elderly witch. "Do close the door, will you, Blair?"

Teeth gritted, I closed the door and locked it for good measure. There was nothing to be done for the dark circles under my eyes, but with the help of a spell, I managed to get most of the cat hairs off my skirt and top. With my hair tied back to hide the frizziness, I looked almost presentable.

"You're dressed for a date," Aveline remarked when I came out of the bathroom. "Who is it, a local wizard?"

Grace laughed. "Look at her blushing. It's probably a mole shifter. Or a weasel."

I scowled. "No, he isn't."

Aveline hooted with laughter. "Werewolf, then? No, they're far out of your league."

I chewed the inside of my lip to avoid commenting that a Head Witch who'd managed to lose her own sceptre had no business telling me who was and wasn't out of my league.

"Please let your daughter back into the house," I said. "You know, if both of you tried to act your age, then maybe we'd all get along better."

"I did my growing up," Grace said. "It's not worth the investment."

I left the witches cackling with laughter and opened the flat door, tripped over the threshold and tumbled into Nathan. He caught me before I fell. "Whoa, Blair. Are you okay?"

A fresh wave of laughter came from behind me.

"He's already swept you off your feet, has he?" Aveline's voice drifted overhead. *Oh, shut up, you old bat.*

Nathan peered past me into the flat. "Is there a problem?"

"She's right, he's not a wizard," Grace said. "What's with the shoes? Did you steal them from a bridge troll?"

All eyes momentarily went to Nathan's boots, which were designed for hiking through thick mud.

"Not quite," he said. "I'm leader of Fairy Falls's security team. I make sure nothing gets in here that isn't supposed to."

Too bad grouchy Head Witches didn't fall into that category.

"You're welcome to escort me home," said Aveline. "I'd even pay for the opportunity."

"Mother!" Vanessa took the opportunity to slip back

into the house. "Who are you hassling this time?"

"This delightful young man has come to take Blair out," said Grace.

Her eyes took in Nathan, and an appreciative look came over her. I pointedly stepped into the way. "I'm going out. If anyone needs me, leave a message with my cat."

Nathan frowned sideways at me as we left. "Your cat? Can he understand messages now?"

"No, and he isn't even in." I rubbed my tired eyes. "That sounded better in my head."

"They don't look like they're doing much searching for the sceptre," he remarked.

"Nope," I said. "I'm guessing the Head Witch has taken Grace and her daughters off the suspect list. I can't believe she got pink hair dye all over my shower."

Nathan's brows shot up. "Is she the Head Witch? The one with pink hair?"

"No, that was the other one." I dug my hands in my pockets, wishing I'd had the good sense to grab a coat on the way out. "The pink-haired witch is Grace Rosemary. It's the woman with the grey hair and the bad attitude who took over my room and made a mess of my flat. And stole someone's fireplace, too. If we don't stay out all night, I'm sleeping in the garden."

"And there I thought you were happy to see me," he said. "You're blushing. It's cute."

"I'm going to pretend I'm blushing because I'm happy to see you and not because a one-woman force of terror flirted with my boyfriend."

He smiled. "I like it when you call me that."

"It's true, isn't it?" Despite the universe's best efforts to thwart us, things had been going well. Too well, almost. I'd been under no illusions that I'd get to spend a great deal of time with him this week, considering the Samhain ceremony, but one date was enough to make up for the otherwise frustrating day I'd had.

The old witches had one thing right. Guys like Nathan *were* out of my league, in the normal world at least. But the paranormal world's distrust of hunters and my own outsider status had somehow conspired to throw us together, and despite all the obstacles that had landed in our path, I couldn't imagine life without him.

Nathan stopped walking, his arm sliding around my back. I leaned in and met his lips with mine, my arms wrapping around his back, feeling the shift of solid muscle under my hands. Nathan was built like what he was—a security guard and former paranormal hunter who'd chased down rogue werewolves for a living. His dark hair had grown shaggier like he'd neglected to cut it recently.

I released him. "I'll ask Nina to give you a free haircut. It's a wonder you can see where you're going."

He smiled. "I've been run off my feet, what with the ceremony. I came straight here from my shift. Which would explain the boots that woman rightly told me look like they belong to a troll."

"She's talking nonsense," I said. "I like your shoes. Mostly because you're the one wearing them."

He laughed, took my hand in his and we made our way down the darkening street. It was amazing how quickly I'd adjusted to living in a town where everyone walked everywhere. After this, going back to a normal town with cars and public transport would be a major culture shock.

Silence formed a backdrop as we walked, along with the faint crash of the waterfall which was only audible in the quiet of night. The winding streets had always reminded me of a picture out of a storybook—narrow, cobbled roads lined with pubs that my former friends in the normal world would probably describe as *quaint*. No night clubs with sticky floors here.

I halted outside the local bookshop when we passed by. It was closed, but maybe Sky had chosen an empty and freezing shop to sleep in rather than being within a mile of Aveline.

"I doubt he ran away for good," Nathan said when I mentioned this aloud. "Most likely, he'll show up at Vincent's place. It wouldn't be the first time, would it?"

"I guess he might be sulking in a coffin," I acknowledged. "I asked Vincent to contact me if he spots him. Sky knows to avoid the house as long as Aveline is there. Actually, everyone should, if they know what's good for them."

"I agree," he said. "Is she permitted to act however she likes, being Head Witch? Because it sounds like she deserves a stern talking-to at the very least."

"Her prize possession was stolen," I said. "But she was acting awful enough beforehand, and now she's playing Scrabble with three of the suspects. Doesn't seem like she's all that fussed about the sceptre, unless it's an act."

"I haven't had any alerts from the police on the matter," Nathan said, "so I can only assume that the local coven leaders don't see it as a cause for alarm. Do you really think one of the other witches might be the thief?"

"The odds of them being inside the house are stronger than most," I said. "I planned to question everyone, but I'll wait until we're certain Aveline didn't hide the sceptre in my underwear drawer for attention. At this point, I wouldn't put anything past her."

"She already searched your room?" he asked.

"Thoroughly." Despite my bad mood, being with Nathan made a significant proportion of my stress melt away. Inside the pub, we picked out our usual table near the door, while I explained everything I hadn't been able to fit into the text messages I'd sent this morning.

"Are you sure the thief didn't get in while you were asleep?" Nathan asked me.

"I didn't sleep." I tapped the menu to order my food. "Aveline's snoring was so loud that someone might have sneaked in without my noticing, but they would have needed to get her door open without waking her."

A thoughtful look came over him. "I think the woman herself did it. Judging by what you've told me, she enjoys playing the victim."

"I wouldn't have thought she'd want the entire town to assume she couldn't keep hold of her own sceptre." My shoulders slumped. "I'm too tired to think of theories. Rob offered to come and sniff the thief out using his werewolf senses, but we've had people trampling in and out of the flat all day. I doubt he'll be able to isolate the thief's scent."

The food and drinks appeared on the table. I dug in, having been too distracted to eat much today.

"What is it the sceptre can do, exactly?" Nathan asked. "Aside from giving the Head Witch her title."

I put down my fork. "They say it contains enough power to part the veil between this world and the afterlife on Samhain, which is why they pick that day to let it choose a new owner. Other than that, I'm not convinced it's worth all the marching around fields in the cold we've done over the last week."

"I haven't heard about the ceremony being cancelled, so I assume Madame Grey is confident the sceptre will be found before then," he said. "Is there anything I can do to help, other than keep an eye out for Sky? If you find him, he's welcome to stay at my house until Aveline leaves."

That was Nathan—he always wanted to help out, and he always found a way to make me feel better. Too bad even he couldn't work miracles.

"If you can think of ways to stop that mad old witch from destroying my room, I'm all ears."

"I'm afraid all the solutions I can think of are magical ones," he said.

"They still might work if she wasn't the most powerful witch in the house—maybe even in the whole town." I picked up my fork again. "And on top of that, she knew my mother when she was still alive. I was wondering why Madame Grey never told me about her before, but now I get it."

Nathan put down his beer glass. "She did?"

I twirled pasta around my fork. "Yep. I don't know if they were friends. Probably not. She doesn't seem to even like her own daughter."

"And you think she might let you speak to your mother's ghost, using the sceptre?" he asked.

Despite not being a wizard, Nathan was as perceptive as any paranormal I'd met, and more than some.

I shrugged and returned my attention to my plate. "Since I'll never get to meet her while she's living…"

"I'm not about to stop you," he said. "I assume you

know speaking to the dead isn't considered advisable."

"This is different," I said. "The walls between worlds are thinner at this time of year. I wouldn't even think about it under normal circumstances."

I wouldn't at all, in fact, if my dad hadn't put the idea into my head. There was just one slight issue… the sceptre had gone.

"I'm not an expert," he said. "Do you need security tonight in case the thief comes back? Maybe the Head Witch will think twice about giving you trouble if I'm there."

"Even Sky didn't intimidate her." It was tempting, though. "I doubt you'll want to hear Aveline's opinions on the hunters. I assume she hates them as much as she seems to dislike everyone else."

"I'm used to it," he said mildly. "Oh, by the way, Blair, your blouse is inside-out."

You might know it. "Yeah, I didn't get much sleep."

"I noticed." His mouth curled into a smile. "I may be able to procure you a potion which will make you sleep better tonight."

"Alissa said she'd teach me an earplug charm, but I'll go for that, too." I sat back in my seat.

He leaned and tapped a drink on the menu. "I have it on good authority that this particular cocktail will help."

"At this rate, it'll take a bottle of wine to get me through the week." I stifled a yawn, my jaw cracking. "Are you positive you want to keep watch outside the house? Her comments to you earlier…"

"Don't worry about it." He smiled. "I've spent years dealing with unruly werewolves. She's going to have to work much harder if she wants to drive me away."

5

The effects of the cocktail worked so well that I slept right through Alissa's return from her shift at midnight and would have been late for work were it not for the sofa falling out from underneath me. I hit the floor with a thud that sent stars spinning before my eyes and jolted me back to wakefulness.

"Ow." I looked up at Aveline standing over me. She'd levitated the sofa into the air while I was sleeping on it. "What was that for?"

"Are you deaf?" she screeched.

"No." *Maybe I am, now.* My head pounded, my mind feeling fuzzy. "Did another thief break in?"

"Certainly not," she said. "That feline of yours decided to move into my bed in the middle of the night. Look what he did!"

She hiked up her dressing gown to show claw marks on her legs. Oh, no. Sky hadn't run away... he'd taken revenge on Aveline into his own manner. Also, I could have lived a long and happy life without seeing her floral undergarments.

"Ah, sorry." I scrambled to my feet, my head aching. "Like I said, he usually sleeps in my room. I'll find him."

I walked into the bedroom to find Sky stretched out on the bed, legs sprawled out the way he lay when he wanted to take up as much space as possible. He gave me a smug look. "Miaow."

"Thank you," I whispered, giving him a stroke. "I appreciate you not running off either. At this rate, she'll drive both of us into an early grave."

At the sound of footsteps behind me, I added, "Come on, let's get out of here."

Sky jumped off the bed and followed me from the room, hiding behind my ankles when Aveline stalked past. Alissa emerged from her bedroom, blinking sleepily. "What's going on?"

"Are you deaf, too?" Aveline shot at her.

No, just wearing an earplug charm.

"What's the issue?" she asked. "Oh, Sky came back. That's good news."

"No, it isn't," Aveline huffed. "That beast attacked me."

Sky made a quiet growling noise that implied *you haven't seen anything yet.* "Alissa, can you watch him while I get dressed?"

I really meant, 'watch Aveline', but I might have to take Nathan up on his offer to let Sky stay at his house until the madness was over. Assuming he got on with Nathan's cats, which was debatable. He and Roald frequently got into territorial battles over the sofa.

I showered and dressed, emerging from the bathroom

to find a message from Nathan on my phone explaining that he'd been called away during the night to solve an argument at the border between two hot-headed shifters. With a twinge of guilt for letting him stand on guard duty half the night, I ordered him to get some sleep rather than coming back to play security guard. In the meantime, I'd have to drop Sky off at Nathan's house on the way to work if I wanted to avoid him turning the Head Witch into a pincushion.

Aveline watched like a hawk as I came out of the bathroom to retrieve Sky from the sofa. "Don't think I didn't see that boyfriend of yours hovering outside the window last night."

"He offered to watch out for thieves." *Please tell me she didn't try to flirt with him again.* Brawling shifters were nothing compared to Aveline's flirtation attempts.

She grunted. "That won't do any good if the thief's inside the house, will it?"

"You saw me question the Rosemary witches. They didn't steal it, and nor did your daughter. That just leaves Shannon." *And you.* "Do you think Shannon did it?"

"No."

"Then who?" I rubbed my temples. Work today was going to be a trial, but not as much as a conversation with the Head Witch.

Her sharp gaze flickered over me. "Who can tell truth from lies?"

"Me, but I'm not the thief." I tensed as she rose to her feet from the armchair, using a stick for balance she must have picked out to replace the sceptre. "My ability isn't fool-proof. People can omit information, either by accident or otherwise."

She sniffed. "Well, what good is that, then?"

"Good enough that I'm sure the sceptre isn't in the house." If one of the other witches had hired someone to act on their behalf, they must have hidden it elsewhere while Aveline tore the place apart.

I beckoned to Sky to follow me out of the flat, and Alissa came, too. Not a sound came from upstairs or the flat opposite, suggesting the other inhabitants were asleep.

"Are you going to question them now?" Alissa asked in an undertone. "I'm not staying here with Aveline until my shift, but if you think one of them did it…"

"I don't know what to think," I admitted. "If Aveline is behind all this, she knows about my lie-sensing power and she will have accounted for it."

"Miaow," said Sky, in a tone that implied *he* didn't think she was clever enough to do so.

I crouched down to whisper to him, "Did you see the thief come into the flat?"

"Miaow." He shook his head, his whiskers twitching.

Then they must have used a spell. Perhaps a stealth spell in combination with an invisibility potion and an unlocking charm—and those were just basic charms. Any of the witches in the house was capable of casting high-level spells I wouldn't get to in my magical education for years. Then again, Madame Grey must have considered all the possibilities, right?

"What are you two whispering about?" Alissa's brow puckered. "The thief? Did Sky see them?"

"No." I straightened upright. "I'd better head off to work. Nathan offered to look after Sky until Aveline leaves town, so I was going to drop him off there on the way. He already has three cats."

"I forgot," she said. "I saw him outside last night, but he was gone by the morning."

"He went to break up a shifter fight at the border." I grimaced. "I think Aveline chased him off, to tell you the truth. I shouldn't have asked him to play security guard all night, but that sleeping cocktail knocked me out."

"I wondered why you slept through every question Aveline tried to ask you." She glanced over her shoulder. "If you ask me, the reason the Head Witch in such a bad mood today is because she couldn't stand being ignored by both of us."

"Until she tossed me off the sofa." I rubbed my sore neck. "She can't seriously think *I* stole the sceptre."

"I'm not sure that's what she was implying." She frowned. "Unless she's the thief and she's deliberately trying to throw us off the trace. I mean, she's held onto the title of Head Witch for years, and it's possible that she's afraid of losing her position. She might have decided that if she can't have the sceptre, nobody else can, either."

"That does sound like her," I said. "Thief or not, she always has to make everything about her."

"Miaow," Sky said in agreement.

"C'mon," I said to him. "Let's get you to Nathan's. You're not to start any fights with his cats while I'm at work, okay?"

"Have fun," said Alissa. "Will Nathan be stopping by tonight?"

"Probably not, but Rob the werewolf from work offered to come back here to see if he can sniff out the thief. At least if Aveline tries flirting with him, he'll tell her she's wasting his time."

Her nose wrinkled. "Who was she flirting with?"

"Nathan. It was scarring, to be honest." I shuddered. "Can you find a way to distract you-know-who for half an hour or so in case she starts hassling Rob? Nobody deserves to be subject to that torment."

Alissa snorted. "I'll see if I can think of a way to distract the Head Witch if you bring the werewolf over."

"Thanks, Alissa." My phone buzzed with a message from Nathan telling me he'd left the cat flap open and enough food for Sky to share with the other three cats. "What d'you reckon, Sky? Nathan's house or Vincent's place? I know you and Vincent are friends, but it can't be comfortable to sleep in a coffin."

Then again, being a cat, he could sleep anywhere without the need for a magical cocktail. I regretted not starting my day with a double-dose of motivational coffee as I trekked to Nathan's house, though Sky followed without a fuss. He could be placid enough when he wanted to be, provided pointed hats weren't involved.

"I can trust you not to fight the other cats, right?" I gave him a stroke. "Nathan left you some food in there. I'll come and see you later, okay?"

"Miaow." Sky wound around my ankles, demanding another stroke, before slinking through the cat flap into Nathan's house.

One thing sorted. Shivering in the chilly air, I made my way to work. The effects of the cocktail lingered, but I was glad of the huge mug of coffee waiting on my desk when I walked in.

"Thanks, Rob." I sat down and picked up the coffee,

which was at a more drinkable temperature than yesterday. Better and better.

"You're welcome," he said. "How's the old bat?"

"Unbearable." I took a long sip. "I'd rather share a room with Vincent the vampire."

Bethan spat out a mouthful of coffee. "You've obviously never heard a vampire talk in their sleep."

"Speaking from experience, are you?" I put down the mug. "The Head Witch snores, flirts with my boyfriend, starts fights with my familiar, and tips me off the sofa when I'm not quick enough to answer her questions."

"Okay, you win," said Bethan. "Any news on this mysterious thief?"

"Nope." And given the decisive answers I'd received to my questioning, either the thief was never in the house, or the culprit was savvy enough to get around my lie-sensing powers.

"You know you offered to sniff out the thief yesterday," I said to Rob. "Can you drop by tonight? Say, half an hour or so after work?" I'd have to give Alissa enough time to turf Aveline out of the house so he could sniff around without her turning him into a chair.

"Sure," he said. "Has anyone been in your flat since the incident?"

"A few people," I said. "But not in my bedroom, which was where the sceptre was stolen from. I just need to make sure she hasn't made too much of a mess of the place before I let anyone in."

"I'm sure I've seen worse. You forget the pack lives in the forest."

"He has a point." Lizzie flashed me a sympathetic look

across the desk. "I hope you catch the thief so that awful woman leaves you alone."

"Me, too."

Once the workday was over, I headed home, bracing myself to find Aveline had upended the place again. Instead, I found the flat looked much the same as it had this morning. Alissa sat on the sofa, stroking Roald. *I hope Sky got on okay at Nathan's house.*

"Hey, Blair," said Alissa. "The other witches have been with Madame Grey all day, so I fixed things up and moved your suitcase where nobody can touch it. I had to leave the bedroom the same, though."

"At least until our uninvited guest leaves," I said. "Rob the werewolf is coming over in a few minutes. She's not likely to come home in the middle of it, is she?"

"I'll keep an eye out for her," said Alissa. "It sounded like Madame Grey was giving her a stern talking-to."

"Good." I jumped when the doorbell rang. "There he is. Punctual as always."

Sure enough, the blond werewolf stood on the doorstep, wearing his usual grin. "Hey, Blair."

"Hey," I said. "This is Alissa, my flatmate. Don't worry, the coast is clear."

"The Head Witch is terrorising my grandmother instead." Alissa stepped aside to let him enter the flat. "I assume Blair told you all about her?"

"She did," he confirmed, walking into the living room. "Has someone been making potions in here?"

"I think that's Grace's hair dye," said Alissa.

He grimaced. "Nasty stuff. Okay, which is the room the sceptre vanished from?"

"Here." I indicated my bedroom.

Rob walked into the room, sniffed a couple of times, then sneezed. "Is there glitter in here?"

"Ah... yeah, but that's not to do with the thief." *More like my weird fairy magic.* "How many individuals do you smell?"

"You and Aveline, I assume." He sniffed again. "And... a cat?"

"Sky. He's my familiar. Can you not smell anyone else?"

"In the living room, yes, but not in the bedroom." He scanned the room. "Was the sceptre definitely carried out through the door?"

"The window's not big enough to climb out of," Alissa said from the living room.

He sniffed around the window and frowned. "Could it have been disguised as something else?"

"Not while I was looking. I can see through most illusions, and it's a powerful magical object. More powerful than a wand. I'll have to ask Madame Grey for specifics, but she must have considered the possibility."

"Fair enough," he said. "I like the place. Very ambient."

"It was even better before a certain elderly witch upended everything," added Alissa.

"I bet," he said. "You know, there's a potion we use on new werewolves to make them more docile and friendly at the full moon. It stops them from snapping at everyone they see. It sounds like this Head Witch might be in dire need of a dose, from what you've said."

I had my doubts that anything could make Aveline the slightest bit docile *or* friendly. "You mean, a witch potion?"

"What else?" he said. "My uncle doesn't like to broadcast that he buys from the covens, but he finds those particular potions are the only way to get any peace when new cubs first shift."

"Should you be telling me this?"

"Probably not." He gave an easy smile. "It's up to you, but the Head Witch sounds like a terror. I can drop some off at work tomorrow if you like."

"Oh, thanks," I said. "If she tries anything else tomorrow, I might need it for my own sanity."

"Anytime." He walked back into the living room. "Sorry I wasn't much help here. And I'd clean up that dye if anyone comes here who has allergies."

"Thanks anyway." I checked my watch. Running late again. "I have to go to a magic lesson, but I appreciate the help."

Not for the first time, I had to run to the witches' headquarters in my work clothes. At least nothing was inside-out this time. I pushed open the doors and collided with Grace coming the other way.

"Ah, sorry," I said.

"Do you ever look where you're going?" Grace's pink hair was in disarray and her mouth pressed into an angry line that didn't suit her. The questioning from Madame Grey hadn't gone well, then. Before I could say a word, she stormed off, leaving the smell of hair dye behind her. It really was potent. Like oil mixed with carpet cleaner.

Rita was mid-lecture when I walked into the classroom to join Rebecca. The red-haired witch wore her usual array of bangles on her arms, which clacked together when she turned to me. "There you are, Blair. I thought we'd start familiar training today."

"Um… okay." I glanced at Rebecca. "Rebecca doesn't have a familiar yet, right?"

"No. I thought you might help her to choose one."

"Oh, sure," I said. "Um, Sky isn't exactly conventional, though. He's a fairy cat, not a witch familiar."

"You and he are closely bonded in a similar way," she said. "I hoped you could help Rebecca get started with some basic lessons once she picks a familiar."

"What if I don't get picked?" Rebecca said.

"Then it's no big deal," said Rita. "But I think you need the companionship. Better hurry—the familiar shop will close soon. Here."

She handed Rebecca a handful of notes, which the young witch took from her with a nod of thanks.

"How's school?" I asked Rebecca on the way out of the classroom.

"Horrible." Her shoulders hunched. "Having a familiar won't stop the others from teasing me about my mum. I wish I could change my name and move somewhere else."

My heart sank. I knew too well what it felt like not to belong, but I was lucky that I hadn't had to relive my school experience in the magical world. I'd found it easier when I'd hit adulthood and it had no longer been necessary to hide from bullies. Poor Rebecca had a raw deal.

"They'll get over it," I said, hearing the lie in my own words.

"They won't," she said. "You know they won't."

If I were her, I wouldn't believe me either. "What exactly are they saying to you? Because I'm not supposed to tell you to fight back against the bullies, but I know ignoring them isn't always the best course of action." For me, ignoring the bullies had only made them try harder to get a rise out of me.

She shrugged. "They're just saying my mum's a criminal and I'm going to be the same. Whenever anyone tries to be friendly to me, someone always tells them I used my magical powers on them. Then they stop talking to me because they think I'm going to enchant them."

"That's awful," I said. "Who's doing this?"

In my experience, bullies worked in a pack. They were terrified of being caught out alone.

"Three girls," she mumbled. "It doesn't matter. My mum *is* a criminal. And my sister was a bully when she was at school."

"That's no excuse," I said. "I think having a familiar will help, but it's worth talking to your teacher—"

"Please no," she said. "They already say I use my magical powers to make the teachers give me top grades."

"They know that's not allowed, right?" I shook my head. "You're smarter than they are. I bet they don't like *that.*" I hoped to get a smile out of her, but Rebecca's shoulders remained hunched. "Okay, is there a teacher you particularly like? I didn't have many friends when I was at school, but I had great teachers."

"I have nice teachers," she said. "But won't telling them make things worse?"

"Maybe," I admitted. "But you don't want to spend your whole time at the academy miserable because of those people, and your teachers might be able to help. In the meantime, let's get you a familiar."

She dipped her head. "Okay."

We made our way down the high street. I'd never had reason to visit the familiar shop before, but it was a small, pleasant little shop staffed by a wererat called Lucas. The shop's inhabitants were entertaining enough to make it easy to ignore the unpleasant smell of animal droppings. Owls, ravens and other birds flew among the rafters, while cages of fluffy kittens filled one side of the room. Dozens of eyes blinked enquiringly at Rebecca as she approached, a smile breaking out on her face.

"Hello," said the shopkeeper. "Can I help you with something?"

"We're looking for a familiar for Rebecca," I said.

"A cat," added Rebecca.

Lucas moved in front of the cage. "Are you sure? Cats might be popular, but rats and mice are easier to train. Cats tend to have strong personalities."

He might not have met a fairy cat, but he knows what he's talking about.

Rebecca ran her teeth over her lower lip. "Ah. I just, uh, I wanted to fit in at school…"

I leaned in and whispered, "Wouldn't the bullies leave you alone if you send a rat up their trouser legs?"

Rebecca giggled. Then a ginger cat with a face like a squashed tomato padded over and blinked up at her, purring.

"Oh, that's Toast," said Lucas. "He's a little older than most of the others—his last witch returned him to the shop."

Rebecca gave a startled jump when Toast stood on his hind legs to rub his head against her hand. "He wants me to stroke him?"

"Go ahead." Lucas looked between the two of them. "The familiar usually makes the first move."

"Is he—?" Rebecca broke off, dropping her hand. I

tried to give Toast a stroke, but he ducked out of my reach and went for Rebecca again.

"He likes you," I said.

Lucas gave a satisfied nod. "I'm not mistaken, I detect a familiar bond there."

Rebecca stopped stroking the cat. "Bond? What do you mean?"

"The familiar is the first to notice." Lucas nodded to Toast, who was purring happily. He was cute despite his misshapen face. "Then it'll grow stronger as you go through training."

"But do I *have* to take him?" she said.

I inched closer to her and whispered, "He can probably understand every word you say."

She flushed and looked down. "My mum would call him a loser."

"Your mum called *me* a loser of a witch. I still got her jailed for life."

Her mouth twitched. "The others will laugh at me."

"They won't when you master familiar training at twice their speed while their own familiars won't even come when their owners call them," said the shopkeeper.

"I can do that?" she asked.

"Sure," he said. "Toast has had three previous owners. He knows all the basic commands already, so training him should be a breeze."

Rebecca bit her lip. "Do you promise?"

"Of course," said the shopkeeper kindly. "Trust me, those sleek young familiars over there might look prettier, but what matters is loyalty. Like Bree here."

He snapped his fingers, and a large tabby cat padded up to him, rubbing his head against his owner's leg.

Five minutes later, we left the shop, pursued by Rebecca's purring familiar.

"He likes you," I said.

"He's very trusting for someone who got ditched three times." She dropped her voice. "I don't know whether to bring him to school, though. I don't need to give Sammi another excuse to laugh at me."

"Sammi? Is she one of the bullies?"

"Yeah," she said. "Sammi and her friends."

"Sammi as in Madame Grey's granddaughter?" *She* was the school bully? Rebecca's mother *had* tried to unseat Madame Grey from the council, but that was no excuse to bully Rebecca. Kids could be unforgiving, though.

"Yeah." She dug her hands in her pockets. "And her two friends. They're in all my classes. I can't escape them."

Maybe I should talk to Madame Grey. I didn't know much about Sammi. The only time we'd met, I'd accidentally turned her transparent with a botched invisibility potion I'd knocked all over the floor. I wouldn't have thought the granddaughter of the Meadowsweet Coven's leader would turn out to be a bully, but then again, Rebecca was nothing like her sister and even less like her mother.

We reached the witches' headquarters and re-entered the classroom. Rita's eyes brightened as she spotted the purring ginger cat. "Good. You did find a familiar."

"This is Toast," said Rebecca, giving him a stroke behind the ears. "I picked him because nobody else wanted him."

"And he picked her, too," I added.

"The shopkeeper said he's a fast learner, because he's already had more than one owner," said Rebecca.

"We'll try the basics first," she said. "Calling him by name, that sort of thing. Should be simple enough, right, Blair?"

Toast purred and rubbed his fluffy head against Rebecca's hand. If nothing else, it would be good for her to have a friend.

6

An hour later, Rebecca left the classroom in a much better mood, while I stayed behind to talk to Rita about the bullying situation.

"The cat will be good for her," she said. "Having a familiar who's easy to train will remove a lot of hurdles."

"Yes... um, she didn't happen to mention the names of her school bullies, did she?" This needed to be dealt with, but I didn't want to make things worse for Rebecca if I could help it.

Rita waved her wand, returning a stack of textbooks to the cupboard. "Did she tell you?"

"She did, and one of them is Madame Grey's youngest granddaughter. Sammi."

She raised an eyebrow. "Sammi? Are you sure?"

"Rebecca told me, and I trust her word," I said. "I know kids can be cruel, but I didn't want to tell Madame Grey and end up with the other kids being angry with Rebecca for telling tales. It's been a while since I was at school, so I'm not sure how to approach this." The magical world wasn't that different from the normal world, but bullying took on another dimension when the perpetrators carried wands and were several years of magical training ahead of their target.

Rita paused for a moment. "Madame Grey will be very disappointed to learn about her granddaughter's behaviour. She practically raised her, after all. But she'd rather know, I think."

I turned this over in my mind. "I don't want to get too involved, but I'll have a word with her."

I remembered begging my foster parents not to call my teacher when the school bullies were taunting me. When you threw magic into the equation, though? I'd rather deal with the matter before it escalated.

From the quietness of Madame Grey's office, it sounded like the other witches had headed back home—or rather, to my flat.

As I raised my hand to knock, the door opened and Shannon walked out. She mumbled a hello and hurried off with her blond head down and a sheaf of papers clutched to her chest.

I stepped aside to let her pass, and Madame Grey called my name from inside the room. "Blair, is that you?"

"Madame Grey. I needed to talk to you." I entered her office, a cosy room filled with bookshelves and dominated by a large wooden desk. "What were you talking to Shannon about? The theft?"

"Shannon used to be interested in coven magic," she said. "I hoped to learn more about her interest in the position of Head Witch, and I loaned her some of my notes."

"Did you suspect her of stealing the sceptre?"

"I haven't ruled anything out, Blair," she said. "Have

you used your lie-sensing power on everyone who was present in the house at the time of the theft?"

"I have, but nobody admitted to anything," I said. "I also asked Rob from the werewolf pack to see if he could sniff out any thieves, and he said nobody went into the bedroom except for me, my cat, and the Head Witch."

"Your familiar was in the room at the time of the theft?" she asked.

"Yes, but he would tell me if he'd seen the thief," I said. "I only saw Aveline."

Right now, the Head Witch herself sat atop the suspect list. The sceptre's owner was the most likely to know how to successfully steal it, after all. Though it didn't explain why she'd stuck around in Fairy Falls, other than to make us lose our collective minds.

"I've spoken to the others myself," Madame Grey said. "All of them admitted to wanting to have a chance of ascending to the title of Head Witch, but none confessed to the theft."

"Is there another reason they might have wanted it, though?" I tried to read her expression, but it was inscrutable. Accusing Aveline might provoke the Head Witch to take it as an insult. Grace Rosemary seemed the second likeliest thief, yet surely if Aveline suspected her, she wouldn't have happily sat there playing Scrabble with the pink-haired witch and her daughters. Right?

"Oh, countless reasons," she said. "Perhaps the thief had a specific spell they needed the sceptre for, or they wanted to restore their coven to its former glory... or to enact a ritual." Her gaze briefly dropped to the desk, where a book lay open to a double-page spread depicting a collection of unreadable symbols.

"Ritual?" I echoed. "You mean like the one Peter the wizard wanted to use to make himself as powerful as a vampire?"

"Yes, but even more potent," she said. "Peter was working with nothing but his own props. The sceptre is a magical beacon. And at this time of year, it's even stronger than usual."

"Because the veil between worlds is thinner." A chill skittered down my spine. "Um, would Aveline have been able to use the sceptre to help me speak to my mother's ghost?"

I still hadn't figured out if that's what my dad had implied in his last message, but if he had, word of the Head Witch being here in Fairy Falls must have reached him even in prison. Perhaps the pixie had told him.

Madame Grey gave me a stern look. "If we do not return the sceptre to its owner, we will have worse to concern ourselves with than the veils thinning, Blair. We need to find this thief and ensure that they are appropriately punished and the sceptre returned for the ceremony, or else I fear this Samhain will be grim indeed."

Madame Grey is afraid? She'd officially freaked *me* out, too. If neither of us had wrung a confession out of anyone we questioned, then maybe I should just dose everyone in the house with Rob's potion until they felt amiable enough to confess to the crime.

"Is that all you wanted to ask me, Blair?" Madame Grey went on.

"Yea—no, it isn't," I said. "Um, I also wanted to talk to you about Rebecca. She says some people at school are bullying her, including Sammi. I know she's your granddaughter—"

"Sammi?" she said. "The girl probably thinks she's defending her coven against Mrs Dailey and her ilk. I'll have a word with her."

"But—" I broke off. Maybe it was for the best that the situation be dealt with early on before it escalated, but Rebecca wouldn't be pleased with me for interfering if it made things worse. Still, she had her familiar to help her through this rough patch. "I don't want to make things worse, that's all."

She gave me a rare smile. "I understand, Blair. Run along, and if you learn anything new about the theft from anyone in your house, you will tell me, won't you?"

"Of course."

I left her office and headed home, turning the new information over in my mind. Aveline still struck me as the most likely culprit but also the least likely to confess. Maybe Rob's potion would help, though. If I got the Head Witch into a better mood, I might stand more of a chance of getting a confession out of her.

An alarming series of crashing noises greeted me as I unlocked the door to the flat. There, I found Aveline standing in the living room, using her wand to move a group of unfamiliar armchairs around.

"What are you doing?" I asked.

"What else? Arranging the accommodation to my liking." She flicked her wand, and the sofa transformed into a large squashy pink monstrosity that looked like an inflatable marshmallow. "This is all too drab."

"This isn't a holiday rental, it's my home," I said. "I put a security deposit on the place and I'd like to get it back. And did you even pay for that furniture?"

86

"For the next week, this is also *my* home," she said. "Oh, and do shut that familiar of yours up."

"MIAOW," Sky said from the corner. He must have braved the Head Witch's wrath to come home and yell at her for wrecking the place. I moved to his side and picked him up before she turned *him* into a pink sofa, too.

"Madame Grey owns this house," I said ineffectually.

"Madame Grey owns the town. We're guests here." She lowered her wand. "Much better."

"Have you seen Alissa?" I asked, with as much patience as I could muster.

"She took that cat of hers outside," she said. "At least her familiar knows its place."

Sky hissed and squirmed in my arms, suddenly twice the size as he'd been before.

"What's wrong with him this time?" She squinted at him. "Is he *growing?*"

Uh-oh. "He does that when he feels like he's under threat."

Sky growled, low and menacing, as the Head Witch moved closer. "Think I'm a threat, do you?"

"Did you steal the sceptre?" The words escaped before I could stop them. "I mean, pretend the sceptre was stolen?"

Her mouth opened and closed. "You *what?*"

"Miaow." Sky wriggled out of my arms and padded to the door, while I ran after him before she made *me* into a permanent piece of furniture. From the stunned expression on her face, Aveline *hadn't* faked the sceptre's theft, unless her shock was because she hadn't expected me to guess.

Crashing noises sounded from behind me, and I fled through the back door and into the garden.

"Is that you, Blair?" Alissa called from somewhere behind a row of flowering plants. "Has the Head Witch finished redecorating yet?"

"Nope." I made my way over to the bench where Alissa sat in the shade of a large tree, Roald in her lap and a textbook at her side. Sky jumped on top of the textbook and curled up, earning a raised eyebrow from Alissa.

"I didn't see Sky come into the house," she said.

"I think he wanted to make sure she didn't throw away any more of my stuff." It was bad enough she'd tossed out my personal collection of bubble wrap. "He half-transformed into his monster form and then I asked if she'd stolen the sceptre herself, so I guess I'm living in the garden now."

Her eyes bulged. "What did she say?"

"She didn't. I ran out here before she turned me into a futon." I glanced over my shoulder at the house, but my bedroom window appeared to be closed this time.

Alissa lifted Sky off her textbook and closed it. "If you ask me, that she's still alive and kicking is proof that she had something to do with the sceptre's disappearance."

"Maybe." Sceptre or none, odds were, if Aveline continued as she was, someone would bump her off before the week was up anyway. Unless I asked Rob for that werewolf potion. "Want to go to the pub until she calms down? Assuming my familiar doesn't commit murder while we're gone."

"I thought he was at Nathan's," said Alissa. "But yeah, sure."

"So did I." I laid Sky down on the ground at the foot of

the bench. "You didn't terrorise Nathan's other cats, did you?"

"Miaow," said Sky, his tone neutral.

I checked my phone but found no new messages from Nathan. Perhaps he was breaking up another brawl at the border. Just my luck. Still, if I couldn't have a date with Nathan, a girls' night out would more than compensate.

Alissa stood, tucking her textbook under her arm. "How did your lesson go?"

"Not too bad. I helped Rebecca get her own familiar, and I think we're going to start training them together." I indicated Sky, who yawned.

"Are you sure he'll behave?" she asked.

"Sky behaves when it suits him," I said. "I'd like to unleash him on Aveline in his monster form right now, to be honest. Anyway, Rebecca adopted a ginger cat who's been ditched by a couple of apprentices already."

"Poor thing," she said. "That's good, then. I heard she was having trouble at school."

"Yeah." Too late, I remembered Sammi was Alissa's cousin. "Did Madame Grey tell you that?"

"She mentioned it." Alissa approached the back door, beckoning Roald to follow her. "Looks like the Head Witch left your room alone this time."

"Don't speak too soon." I risked a peek inside through the back window. Aveline didn't seem to mind that everything in my room was covered in glitter, but I'd rather take a bath in the stuff than let her stay another week. I hardly believed she had the nerve to get rid of our furniture, too. As for where she'd got the replacements from...

Right. I'm going to give her the potion as soon as I get back from work tomorrow.

Alissa and I went upstairs to pick up Nina, then we all headed to the pub together.

"I've been making excuses to stay outside all day," Nina admitted as we walked down the high street. "What was she even doing in your flat?"

"Ensuring I'll never get my security deposit back." I led the way into the pub and ordered a cocktail by tapping the menu.

"My grandmother won't charge you for the damage she does, don't worry," said Alissa, taking a seat opposite me. "She knows perfectly well what the ghastly woman is like."

"Does nobody on the council like her?" Nina perched on the remaining seat. "Is that why someone stole the sceptre—not to use it, but out of contempt for the Head Witch."

"I doubt it," I said. "Unless they planned to leave town the next day and never come back."

"At this rate, they'll never leave." Alissa tapped the menu and ordered her own drink. "If the ceremony goes ahead without the sceptre... well, it can't. Most likely it'll have to be delayed until it's found. It's less powerful on days other than Samhain, but it's do-able."

I groaned. "Please don't say that. The only thing keeping me going is knowing she'll be gone by Monday."

"I don't understand how someone could just pick up something that powerful and wander off with it," said Nina. "Doesn't it have security measures built into it or anything?"

"That's why I'm sure the Head Witch knows more than she's letting on," I said. "I mean, she must figure she has free rein to do whatever she likes as long as the sceptre is missing. Perhaps she faked it for that reason."

Our drinks appeared on the table and Alissa picked up her bright pink cocktail. "But you said she looked shocked when you accused her of orchestrating the whole thing."

"She did." I picked up my own drink. "Not sure that counts as a confession. I should bring backup with me next time. And wear a bulletproof vest."

Nina gave a laugh. "It would explain why nobody heard the break-in, at least. Maybe she turned the sceptre into a piece of furniture."

"I wouldn't have thought that would be possible," said Alissa. "My grandmother conducted a thorough questioning of all the witches today, but I can see Aveline wriggling out of confessing the truth. Thanks to the new prison security, we're confident that there aren't any unsavoury characters in town."

"That's good news," Nina said. "I was awake all that night, too. I saw you out the window, Blair, but nobody else. My mother's freaked out about the whole thing and says I should move."

"She does know it's an occupational hazard of living with us, right?" Alissa sipped her cocktail.

"We have almost as high a turnover of neighbours as Dritch & Co does in employees," I added.

"Don't worry, I'm not going anywhere," Nina said. "I might have said differently if it was my flat the Head Witch commandeered, mind."

"I expect most people would." I took a sip of my cocktail. "Would either of you object if I spiked Aveline's drink with a potion the werewolves give their cubs to make them less grumpy at the full moon? Rob offered to bring some to the office tomorrow."

Alissa tilted her head. "Given how she's acting right now? The whole town would cheer you on. Sounds like the same potion we use on shifters at the hospital if they're acting out and frightening the staff. It can turn a full-grown werewolf into a cute and cuddly puppy."

"I think it's the only way we'll survive this. Though I doubt anything could turn her cute and cuddly." I gave a shudder. "But maybe if she's in a better mood, she'd be more inclined to confess to faking the sceptre's theft. If she's wise to my lie-sensing abilities, we'll need her to loosen up to be in with any chance of learning the truth."

A sudden hush fell over the pub, and everyone turned to the door as Madame Grey strode in, her cloak billowing behind her and her snowy white wand in her hand.

"Alissa, Blair, come with me. You too, Nina."

Alarmed, I jumped to my feet. "What's going on?"

"There's been a murder."

My stomach lurched. "Who?"

"Grace Rosemary." She beckoned imperiously for us to follow her, and we did, without a word. *Grace? She's Aveline's friend.* Unless my accusation earlier had pushed her over the edge.

We hurried after Madame Grey, into the house and through the hallway to the open back door. There, a body lay in front of the rows of herbs, silent and still.

Grace Rosemary was dead.

"When... when did this happen?" The bright pink of her hair looked even more unreal than usual, and I had to remind myself to blink and look away.

"Not long ago, if it was after we left." Alissa crouched down next to her. "Have you checked the cause of death yet?"

"Inconclusive," said Madame Grey. "But there isn't a mark on her. That suggests magic was used—dark magic."

Like the sceptre. A chill ran down my spine. The killer might even have been in the garden at the same time as Alissa and me. Being in the same house as a thief was bad enough, but a murderer was something else entirely.

Footsteps came from behind us. Then a scream. "YOU!" howled one of the twins, who wore a pink dress today. "You did this." She waved a finger at Madame Grey. "Your household murdered my mother."

"Don't be absurd," said Madame Grey. "I received a call from Shannon when she found the body."

I spun around as she pointed towards the nearest bench. I hadn't seen the blond witch, sitting there watching the scene unfold. "Where is Aveline? Still in the flat?"

"She isn't answering the door," Madame Grey responded. "Patience—watch out. You're trampling on a crime scene."

"She's our *mother*," hissed Patience. "Whoever did this, their coven will pay dearly."

She whirled on the spot, slamming into the house. I heard her hammering on all the doors. When she returned to the garden, accompanied by her twin, her eyes were streaming and her expression was livid.

"Dead," said the other twin, who wore blue. "Who did this?"

"Someone who wants to risk the wrath of the Rosemary Coven," Patience said, rapping on my bedroom window with her wand.

"What the bloody hell do you want?" Aveline shouted from the other side of the glass.

"Grace is dead. I was starting to worry you were, too." I stepped closer to the window. "Where is your daughter?"

"I sent her out to get me a new walking stick. This one is too short."

So she wasn't at home. That leaves Shannon, Aveline herself, and Grace's own daughters as the potential suspects.

There came the sound of footsteps, punctuated by Aveline's loud complaints that her hip wouldn't stand for charging around like this. Then she emerged from the house, leaning on the carved stick she'd been using earlier.

Madame Grey attempted to approach the body, only to find her path blocked by the twins. "Charity... Patience, please move aside. We need to determine the cause—"

"We know the cause." Patience straightened upright, jabbing her wand at Aveline. "Murderess! I saw you reeling in her mother with your flattery and your lies."

"She's dead?" Aveline pulled out her wand and pointed it at Grace's body.

Both the twins leapt at her with exclamations of outrage. "You murdered her."

"I did not," Aveline said.

True. "She didn't," I said, then shrank under the twins' punishing glares. "Dark magic killed her. Right, Madame Grey?"

"Correct, Blair," she said. "If I may examine the body—"

"You'll do no such thing." Charity spun on the spot to

face Alissa's grandmother. "Is this how you show hospitality here in Fairy Falls, murdering our coven leader?"

"Watch you aren't next," remarked Aveline. "Don't think I haven't heard you gossiping about the inconvenience of putting up with a coven leader who won't die. My daughter says much the same."

Alissa's eyes bugged out, matching my own expression. *They can't have murdered their own mother, can they?* The twins hadn't tripped up my lie-sensing power when I'd tried to find out who'd stolen the sceptre, but it was an unlikely coincidence that Grace had shown up dead a day later.

"Aveline, you're being absurd," said Madame Grey. "I suggest you all take a moment to calm down before pointing fingers. I, however, intend to call the police."

Great. Just what we all need... gargoyles in the garden as well as vengeful witches.

"Calm down?" Aveline gave the twins a withering look. "I bet I was next on your list, wasn't I?"

Charity narrowed her eyes at her. "Keep pointing your wand at me and you will be."

"ENOUGH," Madame Grey boomed, loud enough to startle Shannon into falling off the bench. "Did you kill your mother?"

"No!" chorused the twins in scandalised tones.

"Not lying, are they?" Aveline turned to Shannon, who scrambled to her feet. "Or is the person who found the body the real murderer?"

"No, I'm not!" Shannon's voice was high, shrill. "I was sitting out here minding my own business when I saw a flash of light. I ran over to the house and found her lying there, dead."

"Flash of light?" said Madame Grey. "Purple light, was it?"

"I can't be certain, but I think so." Shannon visibly trembled. "I didn't see the killer."

"How convenient." Aveline sniffed. "Our lie-sensor is awfully quiet. Not omitting information yourself, are you, Blair?"

"No," I said. "She's not the killer."

"Blair was with us at the pub," said Alissa. "The only people in the house were you—and Aveline. Patience, Charity, when did you realise your mother was missing?"

"Ten minutes ago," said Charity. "She likes to take a walk at midday."

"Liked," said her sister. "Before one of you *murdered* her."

Madame Grey took a step forward. "I must examine the body with the help of a forensic team—"

"You'll do no such thing," Patience insisted. "She's our mother. She will be taken back home where we will deal with her with the proper *respect*."

"I thought you wanted justice," said Aveline.

Patience narrowed her eyes. "Yes, I do. Maybe you had an accomplice commit the deed. Only the sceptre can have done such a thing."

Madame Grey shook her head. "There are other spells… poisons… certainly methods that would be open to any highly gifted witch or wizard."

"You seem to have given this a large amount of consideration," said Charity. "Maybe you had a hand in it yourself. Your enemies do have a habit of disappearing, don't they?"

I stifled a gasp. Now she was accusing Madame Grey?

The air chilled, while Alissa's alarmed expression matched my own.

"If you mean Mrs Dailey, she's safely locked away in jail," said Madame Grey, her face carefully blank. "Those who try to usurp my position have committed a criminal offence, so yes, they are jailed. Would you prefer them to walk free? Or perhaps you have considered committing a similar offence yourself?"

Charity's mouth opened and closed a few times like a goldfish, then she and her twin looked away. "The title of Head Witch is a coveted one. As this is your first year…"

"You thought I shirked my duties as a host to start murdering my competition?" Madame Grey shook her head. "The police will question the witnesses—"

"There was only one witness," said Patience, eyeing Shannon. "Who might have committed the crime."

"I have no quarrel with your coven," she said. "And the Head Witch position is frankly not worth risking my life. I intend to leave the town and travel home tomorrow."

"Guilty conscience?" Patience turned on Madame Grey. "If she leaves and takes the weapon with her—"

Madame Grey's mouth pressed together. "I'm afraid that until the killer is caught, I must ask you to stay put. All of you."

Charity's eyes darted around our group. "The culprit is here among us. If any of you leave town before we sniff you out, we will take it as a declaration of war against our coven."

Shannon sank onto the bench again, her face milky white. Not guilty—but then, who was? The killer had sneaked in and out of the garden like a ghost. Like, in fact, the thief.

"Go," said Madame Grey. "I will check the scene for contamination. Blair, might I ask you to question everyone who was present in the house more thoroughly?"

Patience looked defiantly at me, as did Charity. A definite sense of wariness showed in their expressions. Were they worried about my lie-sensing power because of the murder, or did they have something else to hide?

One way to find out.

7

"Did you see Grace today?" I faced Shannon across the bench, figuring it was best to start with the person least likely to bite my head off. "When was the last time you spoke to her?"

"At Madame Grey's place," the blond witch answered promptly. "She left early, saying she didn't sleep much last night and that she wanted a nap. I think I kept her awake when I was sleep-talking."

Thanking the cocktail that I hadn't been awake through that, I recalled my run-in with Grace earlier. Shannon's account seemed to fit with what I'd seen of the pink-haired witch. "So you stayed at the witches' head-quarters after she left?"

"For another hour, yes," she said. "Then I came back here and decided to sit outside in the garden for a while. It's too stuffy indoors."

More like too full of Aveline. Still, my lie-sensing power didn't react to her words. "Okay, thanks for talking to me."

I turned to the twins next, who both narrowed their eyes at me. *Don't look at me, it was Madame Grey's idea.*

"When did you first notice your mother was missing?" I asked the twins.

"Half an hour ago," Patience said sourly.

Lie. I stiffened. "Are you sure?"

Her twin dabbed at her eyes. "Of course we're not sure. You're interrogating us and she's just lying there on the ground..."

"Madame Grey did offer to move the body."

"Nobody touch her," Patience spat. "Not until the police get here."

I had my doubts she'd let Steve or his fellow gargoyles touch the body either, but I pressed on. "Do you know anyone who would have wanted to harm her?"

"We might have had our arguments, but we're family," said Charity. "We would never hurt one another."

True. "Okay. Unless Vanessa has a confession to make, it seems we have ourselves an invisible killer."

Aveline grunted. "Can I go back inside now? My hip aches. I don't know what's taking Vanessa so long."

The sound of the front door opening came from inside the house, and all eyes turned in that direction.

"I believe that's her now," Madame Grey said.

Alissa disappeared into the house first, and I heard the murmur of voices in the hallway. Then she and Vanessa came outside.

"What's going on?" said Vanessa. "Mother, why are you out here in the garden? You know how your allergies act up around lavender."

"Grace is dead," said Aveline. "And you're the only remaining suspect."

Vanessa gasped. "I've been gone for the last hour. You can't possibly think I—"

"Blair?" said Madame Grey.

I blinked in surprise at having the reins handed over to me. "When was the last time you saw Grace?"

"When she left Madame Grey's office, of course," said Vanessa, her voice tremulous.

"True," I said. "You didn't see anyone else here who shouldn't be?"

"No, of course not," she said. "I've been out for most of the day."

True.

Several gargoyle-shaped shadows appeared overhead. *And here come the police.*

"Steve knows we weren't here when it happened, right?" I asked Madame Grey. The grumpy gargoyle was not my biggest fan.

"Yes, he does," said Madame Grey. "I'd suggest you return to the house in any case."

"Wise idea," Alissa muttered. "I wouldn't put it past Steve to pin the blame on us to avoid ticking off the Head Witch."

"Nor me." I followed her and Nina back into the house. "So we have either an invisible killer running around or one who can commit murder without leaving a trace behind."

"Or someone put a curse on Grace and set it to go off later," Nina added. "Which Steve wouldn't guess, so we'd better hope the Rosemary witches let Madame Grey examine the body."

"I did try a few spells on her when they weren't looking," Alissa whispered. "Enough to figure out that it must have been dark magic that killed her, but a rare type, and not one I've seen before."

"I feel so secure sleeping close to the murder site," I said, with a shudder. "Even camping outside isn't appealing now, to be honest."

"It's okay, you can stay upstairs in my living room if you like," said Nina. "There's more space, and no Head Witch. It's up to you."

I smiled at her. "Might take you up on that. Thanks so much."

In an improved mood, I packed my suitcase and carried it upstairs into Nina's living room. Her flat looked much like mine had before Aveline had unleashed her personality all over it. And it didn't contain any Head Witches, alive or dead, which was a bonus.

Or any murderers.

———

Work was a trial the following day. I'd found it almost impossible to sleep the night before, so I kept dozing off at my desk. My mind had spun in circles, running over every detail of the questionings, but I couldn't figure out how any of the witches might have avoided confessing.

Having a potential killer in the house didn't encourage restful sleep. It was far from the first time I'd been targeted by a murderer—and this time, I wasn't even a direct target. No, all the signs suggested someone was committing murder using the Head Witch's sceptre.

The twins had eventually surrendered their mother's body to Madame Grey for examination, but since Dr Appleton had faked his own death using convincing magic, the process for evaluating the cause of death took longer. Until then, we could only assume the sceptre was responsible. The one bright spot was that Aveline had made such an impact on Steve and the other gargoyles that he'd limited our questionings to less than ten minutes and then flown home.

I'd all but forgotten about Rob's offer to give me a bottle of the werewolf potion until he approached me as work finished for the day and handed me a small bottle. "Two drops will suffice. Just make sure she doesn't see you."

"Goes without saying," I said. "Thanks for this. You might have saved all our sanity if it works."

"I do my best."

I pocketed the bottle, and my phone buzzed with a message from Alissa, telling me that Madame Grey had called another rehearsal for Samhain's event that evening.

Wonderful.

———

Sky had slept on my head while I was staying in Nina's living room, so I hurried home to fetch him before making my way along the winding path to the lake.

Madame Grey waited on the shore, her cloak swirling around her ankles and her white wand aglow as we gathered around her.

"Silence!" she said to the assembling crowd. "You might have heard the sceptre was stolen from the Head Witch this week. However, we have decided to go ahead with the ceremony as planned, to show these thieves that we will not allow them to intimidate us."

What's she playing at? How was it possible to hand on the title of Head Witch without the sceptre? Unless she was planning to use the ceremony to draw the thief out of hiding. Who knew?

To nobody's surprise, the rehearsal didn't go well. Sky was in one of his moods, forcing me to carry the pointed hat myself and nudge him along whenever he curled up stubbornly on the grass. It'd rained overnight, and as a result, walking in the grassy hills was like trekking through a swamp. Regardless, somehow Sky managed to find a dry spot of earth to sleep on every few feet.

When three students started a fight, Madame Grey halted the procession and went to intervene. The rest of us stood shivering on the hillside, damp and miserable, until she dismissed us.

Sky yawned and padded away down the muddy path. I hurried to catch him up and halted at the sound of raucous laughter from the academy students further down the line. Among the laughs, Rebecca's voice drifted over. "Leave him alone!"

Oh, no.

Rebecca stood in a defensive pose among the other witches. At her feet sat her new familiar, curled protectively in front of his witch. Sky padded towards her on silent paws. I didn't stop him, but I followed close behind.

"That idiot familiar of yours was walking in the wrong direction," snickered one of the girls. "Is he too stupid to tell left from right?"

"Well, they do say sometimes familiars take after their owners," sneered a blond girl. "Or the other way around."

"Shut up," Rebecca said, her voice brittle. "He's not stupid. At least I *have* a familiar."

"I'd rather wait for a good one than settle for that mangy old thing," said Sammi. "Did your mum give it you as a punishment for failing her?"

"What?" said Rebecca, her voice catching. "What do you mean by that?"

"Duh, your mum wanted you to turn everyone in town into your personal servants," put in the first girl. "You failed, so she kicked you out."

Their blond companion laughed. "Look at the pathetic thing, he's hiding behind you. Pity he's too fat to hide. What are you going to do when it's time to ride a broomstick? You'd never get off the ground."

They all laughed.

"At least I know how to fly," Rebecca shot at them, picking Toast up. "He's not fat, he's just fluffy. Like you have big heads but no brains to speak of."

"Don't talk to me like that." Sammi pulled out her wand. "You told on me to my grandmother, didn't you? You little sneak. See how you like your familiar now."

She pointed her wand at both of them, but Sky got there first, butting into the back of Sammi's legs. Her wand slipped, and the spell hit one of her friends instead. Sammi fell into the mud with a shriek of dismay.

"Did you do that?" The girl got to her feet, her face flushing, glaring at Rebecca. "I'll show you—"

"MIAOW." Sky positioned himself in front of Rebecca and Toast.

"Everything all right over here?" I gave up on my stealthy approach in the hope of stopping Sky from terrorising everyone with his monstrous form. Even if the bullies *did* deserve a wakeup call.

"Aren't you the fairy witch freak?" said the blond witch. "Sammi said you turned her transparent."

"She did," said Sammi.

"It's true," I said. "Leave Rebecca alone."

"She started it," said Sammi. "She and her mother tried to get my grandma kicked out of town. She never should have been allowed into the academy."

"Rebecca was manipulated. It wasn't her fault," I said.

Sky gave Toast a sniff. He walked around him, once, twice, then he bared his teeth at the other witches. The blond witch got out her wand.

"He bites," I warned. "He's also the one who took out Peter the wizard, so I wouldn't use magic on him."

"No way," said the blond witch. "Is she right, Sammi?"

"Sammi?" Madame Grey called from the other side of the crowd. "Come on."

Shooting Rebecca a venomous look, she stalked off, her friends following suit.

With trembling hands, Rebecca set down Toast at her feet. "Thanks," she mumbled, then ran off before I could reply.

I had the sinking feeling I'd only made things worse. I'd hated it when nobody had stood up for me at school, but Sammi had a grudge and a half against Rebecca's family. Until she dropped that grudge, getting through to her would be difficult at best.

When Alissa and I got home, we found the house deserted. Suspiciously so.

"Where are the others?" I walked into the hall, marvelling at the blessed quietness of the Head Witch's absence.

"I think my grandma mentioned taking them out for dinner after the rehearsal." Alissa unlocked our flat door,

WITCH OUT OF TIME

yawning. "So we have the flat to ourselves. I kind of want an early night, to be honest."

"So do I." I walked into the living room, remembering belatedly that I'd left my suitcase up in Nina's room. "I guess non-coven leaders aren't invited to this dinner."

She arched a brow. "You want to go to the same place Aveline is?"

To spike Aveline's drink with the werewolf potion. Then again, if I got caught, I might well be accused of trying to poison the Head Witch. I'd been lucky to escape a grilling from Steve today as it was. "No, but I'd have liked to solve this sceptre business. If someone in our house stole it, might they have hidden it in their room?"

Probably not, given Aveline's thorough search of the place, but you never knew.

"Good point." She discarded her coat and hat, scanning the living room. "I'll check Aveline's room first."

"You mean, mine." I removed my own coat and went to leave some food for the cats. Sky had taken up his usual position on the sofa with an air that suggested that Aveline would have to pry him off with both hands if she wanted him to move. "I think we'll have to decontaminate the place when she's gone. Is Aveline still leaving clumps of hair all over the shower?"

"Ugh." Alissa shuddered. "I can't get that dye off the walls either. I keep thinking Grace's ghost is going to walk up to me. Pink hair and all."

"Thank you for that mental image," I said. "I'm never sleeping again. It's bad enough that any of us could be next."

"I know." Alissa backed out of my room. "No sceptre, but she wouldn't have left it in such an obvious place.

Besides, she's turned the place inside-out enough times since she moved in."

"You're telling me." I checked the kitchen cupboards, then peered into the bathroom. "Is Nina upstairs?"

"Yep," Alissa said. "I'll check the flat next to hers."

"And I'll check the other downstairs flat." I gave the living room one last scan, willing my fairy senses to show me anything out of place. Aside from the giant marshmallow-coloured sofa, that is. And Grace's hair dye. She'd even left a bottle of it in the bathroom. Grimacing, I tossed it into the bin.

Sky got up and followed me as I left the flat, reaching up with his paws to bat at my pocket. I found the bottle of potion Rob had given me and removed it.

"Hey, Sky," I whispered. "Can you sneak in there and put two drops in Aveline's drink? It's a potion to make her more friendly and relaxed. Considering she already suspects me of plotting against her, I shouldn't push my luck. You're stealthier than I am."

Sky meowed smugly at the flattery and took the potion bottle in his mouth. After the fuss he'd kicked up at the ceremony rehearsal, his lack of argument proved he was as keen to bring Aveline under control as I was.

Now all we had to do was find a killer. Preferably without running into Grace's ghost. Why had Alissa had to go there? I was jumpy enough already.

I accessed the other flat using an unlocking spell but found no signs of the sceptre in any of the rooms. Someone had made the 'borrowed' fireplace disappear, at least. If only they'd do the same for the giant pink sofa which took up half our living room.

I jumped at the sound of footsteps. *Calm down. Ghosts*

can't make a noise, right? Exiting the room, I found Alissa coming downstairs.

"Nothing up there," she said. "The Rosemary witches are neat freaks, compared to Aveline. The place is spotless."

"Even Grace's room?" I asked, thinking of the dye all over the bathroom walls.

"I guess her daughters cleared out her room," Alissa said. "Maybe we can convince Shannon or Vanessa to move upstairs so you can have your room back."

"I'm not so keen to sleep next to the ground-floor window with a killer wandering around, funnily enough." I shook my head. "Why is Madame Grey going ahead with the ceremony instead of looking for the killer?"

"Because the twins are refusing to let her get involved." Alissa's mouth tightened.

"They're threatening to bring in their own coven members to lead the investigation, which would imply to everyone involved that our town isn't capable of handling crime investigations."

"Why do that? We all know the thief hasn't hidden the sceptre in the house, and anyone from outside town wouldn't know where else to look." I tensed at the sound of the door opening, but it was only Sky, slipping back into the hall. He purred to let me know that he'd delivered the potion as promised. Now all we had to do was wait for the effects to kick in.

"Blair, you look shifty," said Alissa. "What are you and Sky plotting?"

"I may have asked him to slip Aveline the werewolf potion."

She frowned. "How much?"

"Uh… I didn't say." Oh, no. I'd forgotten to be specific. "You didn't put in the whole bottle, did you, Sky?"

He offered me the bottle with a muffled meow. I felt it. Lighter than before… but by more than two drops. Oops.

"Don't worry, it's not dangerous," Alissa added. "She might be extra serene, but that'd be an improvement all around."

I hope so.

8

I'd hoped for a restful night, but it was not to be. Aveline retired to bed upon her return to the house, leaving me with the hope that if the effects of the potion kicked in overnight, it wasn't obvious that any outside force was responsible for changing her mood. Yet despite the silence, I tossed and turned so much that Sky climbed off the sofa, fed up with me dislodging him.

"Did I do the right thing?" I whispered to Sky.

"Miaow." He yawned, then crossed the dark floor of Nina's living room to the window.

Yawning, I moved to his side. The night was dark and gloomy, yet someone stood in the garden beneath the window.

Aveline.

I grabbed my shoes and shoved them on, then hurried downstairs as quietly as I could manage. Holding my breath, I eased open the back door and walked out onto the stretch of grass behind the house.

Aveline turned and smiled at me. "It's a beautiful night."

My mouth fell open. *Wow, that potion worked well.* Problem: she was supposed to be happily sleeping, not wandering around the garden when someone had been murdered not five feet away.

"Uh… I guess it is." It was also cold and damp. "Grace died out here, Aveline. It's not safe to wander outside until the killer is caught."

"Grace will be fine."

"Uh, not really. She's dead." I looked around. "I don't think you should be alone out here."

"I'm a big girl. I can take care of myself."

Yeah, but you lost the sceptre. She didn't even have her wand out. Her hair hung loose, and her features looked much less harsh and beaky without the perpetual scowl on her face.

Maybe I'd made a mistake. The others were bound to notice the difference in her manner. I could only hope that their dislike of Aveline's usual personality would prevent them from confronting Alissa or me about the potion.

"Please come back inside." I wrapped my cold arms around myself, wishing I'd grabbed a jacket. "There'll be plenty of time for you to take a walk outside during the day."

"There is no time quite like the space between night and day," she said. "It is a liminal time, a place of boundaries, especially at this time of year."

"Because the veil between the worlds is thinner?" I asked, curiosity rising despite the lingering chill in the air.

"Is it true that on Samhain, it's possible to talk to the dead?"

"Yes, it is," she said, not taking her eyes off the sky. "With a certain spell."

"What spell?" The words escaped before I could reel them in. *Stop it, Blair. Never mind talking to your mother— you have to get the Head Witch back into the house before someone notices she's gone. Or before the murderer shows up.*

She turned to me. "Not one a novice witch like yourself would know. Who do you wish to speak with?"

"My mother," I said. "Tanith Wildflower."

"Ah, Tanith," she said, her eyes back on the sky. "It's been a long time since I've heard anyone speak of her. Tanith, heir to the Wildflower Coven... the coven died out with her mother, in the end."

Questions exploded in my mind like fireworks. "You knew her? When?"

"I thought I knew her," she mused. "That is, until she was arrested for stealing the sceptre."

My heart dropped somewhere below the earth. "Not *that* sceptre?"

"The very same." She sounded sad, which was downright weird coming from someone who'd made my life a misery for the last week. "She pleaded guilty and handed it right back. Never confessed to why she did it."

And then... and then she'd died. When the hunters had caught up to her. I knew the rest of the story. But I'd hoped they were in some way mistaken about her criminal ways. That she'd had good reason for what she did.

Aveline's words carried the unmistakable ring of truth. There was no doubt.

ELLE ADAMS

I blinked tears from my eyes. "It makes no sense."

Tanith Wildflower had taken her secrets with her to a place I couldn't reach—unless I retrieved the same sceptre she'd tried to steal.

"If she had a reason for stealing it, she never gave one," said the Head Witch. "She pleaded guilty and that was the end of it."

"So was she released?" I asked. "Or did she run away? She must have done, because she met my dad and had a child."

She adjusted her grip on the walking stick. "I understand why she threw the coven leadership away now. Maybe she planned to use the sceptre to protect you."

"Against what?" My heart beat loudly in my chest. *This is impossible. How can my mother have tried to steal something so powerful and dangerous?* "Someone was chasing them. My dad, too. Who was it?"

She shook her head. "She never told us. Your grandmother's heart was broken, you know... I don't think she ever recovered."

"What happened to the sceptre?"

"It was returned to its rightful owner," she said. "Me."

"My mum stole from you," I said. "Is that why you don't like me?"

"Don't like you?" She paused. "Not at all. If anything, I see too much of her in you... you're a disruptive force, Blair Wilkes."

"I don't mean to be," I whispered, blinking hard. "I just want to live in peace and not have to deal with bodies turning up in my back garden."

Her gaze went to the spot where Grace's body had lain. I could swear traces of her pink hair dye clung to the dewy grass. "Grace would be angry that she died in such an undignified manner."

"Well, she didn't exactly choose where she died," I said. "Um, Head Witch, if you don't mind my asking... can you tell me which spell will let me speak to a ghost?"

She tapped her cane on the grass with a squelching noise. "Find a written version of the spell and take it with you, if you wish to attempt it. Don't try to conduct the spell from memory. Far too much potential for disaster. I believe Madame Grey owns the book... I saw it in her office."

"Thank you," I said, surprised to find I meant it. "I never knew my mother, and I only started learning about her when I moved here to Fairy Falls. Do people try to steal the sceptre often?"

"No," she said. "It's not a good thing that it was used to commit evil. I fear it may have some terrible side effects."

She's afraid? That wasn't a good sign. It might be part of her personality flip, but either way...

The Head Witch turned back to the house. "I think I will return to bed."

As she hobbled away from me, I remained still, my gaze on the pink-dyed patch of lawn where Grace's body had been found in our otherwise peaceful garden.

Aveline's answers had only left me with more questions. My mother... well, one thing was for certain, she wasn't the culprit this time around. Dead people couldn't steal things. She must have had good reason for taking the sceptre to begin with. But even Madame Grey hadn't known my mother had stolen from the Head Witch—or she hadn't mentioned it to me, anyway.

A shadow flitted overhead, and the pixie appeared in a swirl of glitter.

"What are you doing here?" I whispered. "Did you hear what Aveline told me? Does my dad have anything to add to his message?"

He'd told me so little to begin with, I doubted it. Did he even know about the Samhain ceremony and the regional witches visiting? Or the sceptre?

The pixie flew in circles, beckoning with a small hand. He wanted me to follow him. Well, I was already awake, with time to kill before work.

The little fairy flew towards the back of the garden, over the fence, and down the darkened street until we drew closer to the route past the lake where the procession was due to march on Samhain. I switched to my fairy form to avoid the slippery paths as the grass turned to soggy marsh. At this rate, we'd have to swim through mud on Saturday rather than walking. I'd heard they'd once tried to conduct the ceremony on broomsticks only for a bunch of students to cause a pile-up, but the mud might be just as hazardous.

Despite the glitter falling from the pixie's wings, he was getting hard to spot in the growing fog. I could barely even see my own hands in front of my face. *What am I doing?* Here I was on a wild pixie chase while the sceptre was missing, along with any chance I might have to talk to my dead mother—

I halted. Several human-shaped blurs appeared in the fog, too indistinct to make out. One of them held a long, thin stick. *The sceptre?*

I tripped headfirst over an unseen rock and landed in

the mud. Spitting out a mouthful, I flew upright, searching in vain for the foggy shapes I was sure I'd seen. A female figure, carrying a sceptre...

No, it can't be. I was just imagining things, thanks to Aveline's revelations. Ghosts didn't... okay, they did exist in the magical world, but that was no reason for my mother to choose now to appear.

That's enough, Blair. Whatever I thought I'd seen, it wouldn't solve any of the town's problems. The sooner we found the sceptre, the better.

———

Once I'd gone back to the house to change out of my muddy clothes, Alissa, Nina and I went out for coffee at Charms & Caffeine before work. None of us had slept much, but I wanted to confide in someone before Aveline's revelations caused me to do something reckless.

I ordered a huge extra-strength coffee, delivered by Lizzie's sister Layla, the original creator of our office's coffee machine.

"So you're going to explain why you were covered in mud this morning?" asked Alissa. "Were you out walking in the fog?"

"Pretty much," I said. "Aveline went wandering outside in the middle of the night and I wanted to make sure she didn't get ambushed by the killer."

Alissa raised an eyebrow. "Did you really?"

"You know she's not... in her right mind at the moment." I fidgeted. "We talked about my mother."

Nina looked at me curiously. She didn't know as much

as Alissa did about my family history, but her involvement in Mrs Dailey's trial had led to her picking up on some of the details. Everyone knew my dad was a fairy, at least. And if the hunters came back, I'd bet word would spread about my mum's supposed criminal dealings. I'd decided to get ahead and tell everyone I knew before the rumours could get there first.

"The Head Witch knew her," Alissa said. "Right?"

"I wouldn't say they knew one another well. Aveline arrested her for stealing—well, for stealing the sceptre. Over two decades ago."

Alissa choked on her coffee. "Are you sure?"

"She didn't lie." I slumped down in my seat. "I know we have more concerning things to worry about, but I can't believe my mother was actually a thief."

"Doesn't mean she didn't have her reasons," said Alissa. "Maybe she wanted to use the sceptre against these enemies of hers."

"I thought the same thing," I admitted. "She and my grandmother were the last of their coven. So when her mother died, that was it. Nobody else survived who might know the truth."

"Sorry, Blair," Alissa said. "If it's any consolation, most covens aren't formed of people who are blood relations. You're still a member of the Meadowsweet Coven if you want to be."

A lump formed in my throat. Sometimes I thought I didn't deserve a friend like Alissa.

"I know all about coven law," added Nina. "It's really not a problem to have you inducted into the Meadowsweet Coven formally when the time comes."

I gave a grateful nod. Nina would understand some of

my situation, because she and her mother had been kicked out of their own coven by Dr Summers, before her arrest, which had led them to set up her own coven from scratch.

"Anyway, the reason Aveline is so talkative is that the potion worked a little too well," I added. "She's actually being *nice*, so chances are, someone will realise I'm responsible for her change in personality."

"Oops," said Alissa. "The potion isn't harmful. I've used a variation on patients before. Okay, it's usually to stop werewolves from eating the other patients..."

I grinned and sipped my coffee. "Pretty much the same thing. As for the mud, I decided to go for a walk in the hills after Aveline went to bed."

"You *decided* to go out in this ghastly fog, even though you have to do the same in Samhain rehearsals every other day?" Alissa shook her head. "That's not all, is it? I know you're freaked out about something, Blair."

She knew me too well. "I think I'm losing my mind, but I saw... a ghost." I looked down at my coffee mug. "She vanished when I got up close, but I could have sworn she was holding the sceptre."

A moment passed. I risked a look up at the others, hoping they didn't think I was losing it.

"You believe me?" I asked.

"Of course I do," Alissa said. "They do say the veil between the worlds is thin this time of year. It's not the first story I've heard."

"Likewise," added Nina.

"In the normal world, everyone would think I was nuts. But I guess ghosts aren't that weird over here." Even after living in Fairy Falls for almost six months, running into the ghost of my dead mother struck me as too far-fetched.

Given the fog, it might have been any old ghost. What had Aveline said? That the sceptre being missing at Samhain might have side effects?

I think we're in even more trouble than I thought.

9

Callie wasn't in the reception area when I arrived at work. A strange man in a business suit stood in her place, staring around the room with an expression of confusion. My paranormal-sensing powers told me he was a wizard, but not why he was here. His suit looked clean, but there was something oddly... shiny about him.

"Uh, excuse me, can I help you?" I asked. "We're not open yet..."

"Who's there?" Lizzie walked out of the office, her brows rising at the sight of the stranger. "Did you want to hire us? I don't remember arranging an appointment."

"My name is Simon," he said. "I live here. This isn't an office."

"Um, I think you've got the wrong house," I said. "This office belongs to Dritch & Co. We're a recruitment firm. Nobody lives here. Except possibly upstairs..." I looked at Lizzie. "Right?"

She nodded. "Yes, there's a tenant upstairs, but this is the reception area."

"We open at nine," I added. "I'm Blair."

He held out a hand to shake and it went right through mine. Now I knew what was odd about him... he was dead.

"You're a ghost." I looked at Lizzie. "Are you seeing what I'm seeing?"

"Yes." She backed towards the office door. "That explains it. Uh, Veronica isn't in yet. Simon, can you stay put?"

At that moment, the door slid open and Callie and Rob walked into the reception area. Neither of them gave the newcomer a second's glance.

"Hey, Blair, Lizzie," said Callie, walking straight *through* the ghost as though he wasn't there. Her brow scrunched up as my jaw dropped. "What's wrong?"

"There's a ghost." I pointed to Simon, who looked utterly outraged that anyone had had the gall to walk through him. "He says he lived here..."

Callie blinked at me in bafflement. "What are you talking about?"

"Can only witches see ghosts, by any chance?" I asked Lizzie.

"Yes," said Lizzie. "Blair's right, Callie. He's standing right there, by the way."

"Really?" Rob looked where she pointed. "Hi, there."

"Are you mocking me?" said the man. "I'm not a ghost."

He turned around and walked through the wall into the office. His loud exclamations drifted out of the door.

"We're being haunted?" asked Callie. "Who is he?"

"Someone who used to live here, apparently," I said.

"When did Veronica turn this place into an office? I think there might have been a door over there." I pointed towards where he'd disappeared, from which disappointed sounds ensued, suggesting he was not impressed with the setup of our office.

"Ask Bethan," said Lizzie. "I've only worked here for four years."

There was a crash from inside the office. "Ghosts can't touch anything, can they?"

"They aren't supposed to be able to." Lizzie hurried into the office—through the door, not the wall—and halted beside the four desks grouped in the centre. A noise that sounded like a cross between a rattle and a hiss came from the printer.

Rob walked into the room behind us. "Is the ghost still in here?"

"I am *not* a ghost," snarled Simon, who stood in the middle of the desk, an expression of outrage on his face.

The printer contributed by making another loud growling noise. Lizzie winced. "I think the printer knows there's someone in here who shouldn't be."

"The printer can see him and I can't?" said Rob. "That's unfair."

"You're all completely mad," said Simon. "This is my house! What is this mess?"

"Hey, it's not that bad," I said. "Rob's tidied the place since he started working here."

Okay, the four desks were still covered with heaps of documents, the printer in the corner threw occasional temper tantrums and the coffee machine looked like it had arrived from the future, but Lizzie's technological creations worked wonders. I'd be a little freaked out if I saw them in my house without explanation, but why had a ghost who'd evidently been buried a long time chosen to show up now?

Lizzie turned on her computer. "Don't worry, we'll deal with this. Um, ghosts aren't really my area, though."

"Can all witches see them?" I asked. "Because it'll be kinda awkward if the boss can't."

"I would have thought she'd be able to." Lizzie's hands raced across the keyboard. "Ghosts aren't that common, and maybe one in three witches have the gift, but there's usually a reason spirits come back from death. Why'd he come back now?"

"I am here, you know," said the man. "I can hear every word you say. This is my home, and I don't approve of this at all. And just what *is* that decorating scheme in there?" He pointed in towards Veronica's office.

"Ah," said Lizzie. "Yes, our boss has an interesting taste in decor."

"That's my living room!" he said indignantly. "You can't just walk into my home and redecorate."

"We don't own the building, we just work here," I said. "Also, if you're dead, you don't own the house any longer."

The printer hissed and spat a wad of ink at him. The ink passed right through the man and splattered all over the wall.

Lizzie sighed. "It's going to be one of those days, isn't it?"

"I hope Veronica can see him, otherwise we're in for a fun time." I waved my wand at the wall, making the ink vanish.

Sure enough, the ghost stormed, or rather floated, around the office for the next hour complaining and threatening to make phone calls. When Rob cheerfully offered him the phone—on Lizzie's instructions—he put his hand straight through it. Meanwhile, the printer took such offence at our supernatural visitor that it printed everything in neon green and made constant growling noises.

When Bethan entered the office, she jumped at the sight of the ghost standing in the desk. "Whoa. Who brought a ghost here?"

"I am *not* a ghost," Simon yelled. "Get these people out of my house."

"It's not your house!" I said, exasperated. "Please tell me Veronica's here. He's driving the printer crazy."

Bethan pressed a hand to her forehead. "My mother's running late, but I think she left some sage in her desk. It repels ghosts."

As she left the room, the printer ejected another wad of paper, which soared through Simon's head.

"How dare you attack me!" he screamed.

"The printer thinks it's defending its territory," said Lizzie.

"Yes, I know it *was* your house," I told the ghost. "But this is a mistake. Do you remember anything before you woke up here? I mean, did someone summon you from beyond the grave?"

"Nobody summoned me," he insisted. "I live here, and I'm going to stay here."

"I'm afraid our boss won't like that," Lizzie said. "Can you please keep it down so we can deal with today's clients?"

"I'll handle the phone," Rob said. "He could scream insults at me and I wouldn't know."

"I wish you *could* see him." Rob was the best of us at dealing with problem clients, but not ghostly ones.

To think I'd assumed work would be the *least* stressful part of my day.

Bethan returned to the office with a bag of sage, which we laid around the room's boundaries. Despite that, the next few hours were punctuated by interruptions from the ghost, and the printer, often at the same time. Rob took all the phone calls, but even then, we ran into problems.

"Wolfton has cancelled," he said. "Apparently, he suffered hysterics after a poltergeist threw a chair at him." He said this as though it was a minor inconvenience, not one of our major clients.

"Seriously?" I said. "A poltergeist—that's like a ghost, right?"

"A powerful one," said Lizzie. "Poltergeists can use magic to move objects around. They often show up in normals' houses, but they often assume they're imagining things."

"In my house at the moment, I'd blame it on Aveline." A chill ran down my back. I'd never been a fan of ghost stories. "Is this happening in other places, then?"

"If you mean ghosts showing up... yes." Rob put the phone down. "I've heard from at least three clients so far who've had restless spirits show up in their houses. Is there a mass exodus from the afterlife?"

The door in the reception area opened, and Bethan sprang to her feet. "There she is."

"Veronica!" all of us called at once. "We need you in here."

The boss walked into the office in time to see the

ghost aim a punch at the printer and fall onto his face. The printer's lid flew open, expelling ink everywhere.

"Oh, hello," Veronica said to Simon. "Can I help you?"

"Yes, you can start by getting those people out of my room!" he snapped. "And who the devil lives upstairs?"

"He's a ghost," explained Bethan. "We covered the place in sage and he still won't leave."

"This is my home!" he said. "I demand you leave at once."

"Well, now, this won't do." She turned to the printer. "Clean up that mess. I'll talk to your visitor. Come with me."

She snapped her fingers at the ghost, and to my surprise, he obeyed. With him gone, I could finally hear myself think. I went to help Lizzie clean up the mess of ink on the wall, while Bethan took the opportunity to pick up the phone and call a client.

"Another cancellation," said Bethan. "*Three* ghosts this time."

"Is there anywhere that *isn't* being haunted?" Lizzie wanted to know. "I should check with my sister to make sure there aren't spirits ordering lattes from Charms & Caffeine and not paying for their drinks."

"It sounds like it's just happening here," Bethan said. "In Fairy Falls, I mean. But there aren't that many witches with the skillset to banish spirits who don't want to be gone."

"Is there not a magical equivalent of the Ghostbusters or something?" I asked.

"What's that?" Rob said.

"A movie from the normal world." Sometimes it was hit and miss what references worked in the magical world. "Who do you usually call in when you have a ghost in the house? An exorcist?"

I'd had one incident involving spirits since I'd moved to Fairy Falls, when I'd met the ghost of a wizard pirate who'd haunted the lake. Once I'd dealt with the issue that was keeping him confined to this world, he'd left willingly. He, on the other hand, had at least figured out he was dead.

"A witch or wizard," said Lizzie. "We learned how to banish spirits in school. But you'd be surprised how many people don't mind sharing their house with a ghost, provided it's mutually agreed upon."

"No thanks," I said. "Having a mad old witch living in my flat is quite enough for me."

"I'm not dead," insisted the ghost, marching through the wall. "How dare you sit here in my own home and gossip about me?"

Despite myself, an unexpected rush of pity went through me. He clearly had no idea how long he'd been gone, and it must be jarring to find a bunch of strangers had taken over his house while he'd been... wherever ghosts went after they died.

"I thought Veronica would have been able to banish him." Bethan looked worried. "If she couldn't do it... I might have to call Madame Grey."

She picked up the phone, but the sound of a dial tone came through.

"Bet she's getting calls from all over town," said Lizzie. "Everyone will want her to come in person to get rid of their unwanted ghosts."

"I'll message Alissa and ask," I said. "Though... if there's a ghost epidemic, I can only imagine how many of them showed up at the hospital. Who can see spirits aside from witches?"

"Reapers," said Bethan. "But they only deal with spirits when they first die, not years-old ghosts."

"Reaper?" I asked. "As in the Grim Reaper?"

"Yes, but the Reaper's job is to take souls into the afterlife for the first time," said Bethan. "I've never heard of them having to deal with an outbreak."

"Has it never happened before, then?" I already knew the answer. Even in the magical world, this ghost swarm wasn't natural. Or the ordinary kind of unnatural, anyway. Ever since my weird encounter in the fog this morning, I'd felt off-balance. Samhain was on the way, and Aveline had implied that stealing the sceptre and using it to kill would have consequences. Consequences like a swarm of ghosts? When the sceptre had been used to commit murder, had it brought down the barrier between worlds?

And if the town's long-dead inhabitants were coming back, might my mother be among them? It might not have been her I'd seen in the hills, but Simon was no hallucination. He was in the office, annoying and undeniably present. It wasn't unreasonable to wonder if my mother wanted to speak to me as badly as I wanted to talk with her.

That's enough, Blair. A plague of ghosts was not good news. The people who might get some joy from being reunited with lost loved ones were outnumbered by those who'd be majorly inconvenienced by having a spirit wandering around their property.

Feeling restless, I got up and left the office. At the back of the reception area, the boss's office door lay open, and within, I glimpsed bright neon pink walls and vibrant modern paintings. No wonder poor Simon had been alarmed at the sight of the place.

"Come in, Blair," Veronica said. "Don't lurk."

I stepped into the room. "Hey, Veronica. I wanted to have a word with you about the ghosts."

She looked up from her desk, where heaps of strong-smelling herbs lay scattered. "The sage ought to have sent that spirit packing. How vexing."

"Uh, about that," I said. "You know the sceptre was stolen, right? Might that be why there are ghosts showing up? They say the veil between this world and the afterlife is supposed to be thinner at this time of year, and it might have… side effects."

"Side effects," she repeated. "Yes… I think you're right. The ghosts may indeed be connected to the missing scep-tre. I'm afraid I don't know if Madame Grey has made any progress on finding it yet."

"Nor me. Bethan can't get through to her on the phone, so I guess everyone's calling and asking her to help get rid of the ghosts." One extra ghost in our office was disruptive but not a cause for concern, but when you multiplied it by the number of houses in town, it became a major issue. And what if the newcomers never left? How was anyone supposed to do their jobs with the dead hanging around?

"Since there's nothing to be done, we will proceed as normal," said Veronica. "Do try to ignore the spirit. If he's here because of the veil thinning, then he will be gone by next week."

I opened my mouth and closed it again. Bringing up my mother would do nothing but make me wish for the impossible, and besides, finding the sceptre was more important than filling in the missing gaps in my family history.

When I left work that evening, I walked out into a haze of low-level fog, which masked the road like transparent snow.

Whoa. That's new.

Maybe the fog was also a side effect of the missing sceptre, too. And the eerie silence that filled the streets, as though all the living people had hidden indoors. Shivering from more than the cold, I hurried to the witches' headquarters for my lesson and found a line of people outside, winding all the way down the road. With difficulty, I squeezed past them into the lobby. As I'd suspected, the line halted at Madame Grey's office, but the way to the classroom was clear.

I pushed open the door and found Rita and Rebecca were already there. From Rita's position at the front of the room, she'd opted to ignore the crowd outside and get on with the lesson.

"Did you see all those people?" I sat down. "Doesn't Madame Grey want help dealing with them?"

"I'm a diviner and a teacher, not a ghost expert," Rita said. "I already told everyone to help themselves to our supplies of sage and place it around every room that contains an unwanted spirit."

"We tried it in Dritch & Co's office," I said. "Didn't work. Lucky there was only one ghost."

"Can most people not see them?" asked Rebecca. "Only a few of us in my class could."

"The gift varies," said Rita. "I'm not surprised you and

Blair can both see them. You have a gift for seeing the truth."

"All the witches in my office could, but the werewolves couldn't," I said. "Even the boss couldn't get rid of the spirit, though. She thinks it's a side effect of the veil between worlds being thinner at this time of year, and says the ghosts will all be gone by next week. Do you think so, Rita?" I didn't want to bring up the sceptre in front of Rebecca, who had enough to worry about.

"She's likely right," she said. "Once the week is over, everything should be back to normal."

"But—" I broke off with a glance at Rebecca. There was no point in bringing up my theories about my mother, not yet. "If Madame Grey can't get rid of them, it's going to cause a lot of disruption."

"Not to my lessons," she said. "Turn to page twelve, you two."

I should have known Rita wouldn't let a small thing like a ghost epidemic stop her from getting on with magical theory classes.

We got to work. Occasionally, she looked up and tutted at the sound of voices in the lobby. "They're making such a song and dance out of this. You'd think nobody had ever seen a ghost before."

"They haven't seen hundreds of them at once," said Rebecca. "Is it because the sceptre's missing?"

She was a smart kid. Too smart to be fooled. I turned to Rita. "Do you think so?"

"Get on with your work, both of you. No speculating." Rita grimaced at a crashing noise from overhead. "Ignore the noise. Sammi has a ghost in her room and is refusing to let anyone banish it."

Rebecca flinched at the sound of Sammi's name. "Can they be banished, though? I mean, I know we haven't covered it in our lessons yet, but if Madame Grey can't do it—"

"She can," said Rita. "When it comes to these ghosts, they're likely to go away on their own. There is no point in panicking."

We finished the lesson in silence, and then Rita dismissed us. By now, the queue outside had gone down somewhat, with only a few witches mingling in the lobby. Rebecca came out of the room behind me, and whispered, "Thanks for the other day. I don't know what they'd have done if you hadn't stepped in."

I grimaced. "I'm sorry. I wish there was more I could do to help."

"Some of them are blaming the ghosts on me, too," she said. "Luckily, Sammi can see them too."

Being Madame Grey's granddaughter, it wasn't a surprise that she could. I wished I could make her and the others realise they had more in common with Rebecca than they thought.

"I'll see you at the next lesson," I said. "Oh, how are you getting on with Toast?"

"He's great," she said, brightening. "The other kids tease me about him, but he's great to have around. And he obeys all my commands."

"That's what you want," I said. "Between you and me, Sky isn't a conventional familiar either. He's a fairy cat."

Her eyes rounded. "Really?"

I nodded. "Sometimes it's good to be a little different. Even in the magical world."

10

When Rebecca left, I headed to Madame Grey's office. I wanted to talk to her about Aveline's assertions about my mother stealing the sceptre, just to get the weight off my mind. The queue had almost vanished by now, and after the last witch left the office, I caught the door before it closed.

"Oh—Blair," said Madame Grey in distracted tones. "Are you the last one? I need to speak with Helen—I'll only be a minute."

"Sure." I walked into the office. To my surprise, I spotted Sammi standing in the corner. "Oh, hey, Sammi."

She muttered a hello without looking at me. *Awkward.* I moved behind the desk to wait for her grandmother, while Sammi paced in front of the door. She looked more like Alissa than her grandmother, and perhaps it was that similarity that drove me to say, "I'm not here to tell tales on you again, don't worry."

Sammi turned to frown at me. "You got me into trouble."

Her hand twitched towards her wand. Maybe I shouldn't have brought up the subject, since she had ten times my skill as a witch. On the other hand, she was, well, eleven. And she had good reason to dislike Rebecca's family.

"I thought your grandmother would have taught you not to torment your fellow witches," I said. "Or your parents."

"My mum's dead." Her shoulders hunched. "And my dad left town."

"Oh," I said, surprised. I'd known Madame Grey had raised her, but I hadn't realised it was because her other immediate family was absent. "I'm sorry. I didn't know."

It sounded like she and Rebecca were in similar circumstances, though they might not realise it. "Well, there's no excuse to bully the other students. Especially someone like Rebecca, who's had a rough time of it this year. It's not fair that she has to deal with you teasing her on top of that."

She flushed bright red. "I'm not a bully. Her sister—"

"Her sister bullied *me*, but that doesn't make Rebecca responsible. And her mother was worse."

Her gaze dropped. "She can use magic to change people's personalities. It's freaky."

"Anyone else can do the same with the right spell," I said. "Who told you being different was a bad thing? All of us would be freaks in the normal world."

She blinked. "It's not that she's different. It's just that she's not like... us."

"Do you think *I'm* a freak?" I asked. "Because you'd be agreeing with Blythe if you said yes."

She opened her mouth and closed it. "No. I guess not."

"I'm not going to play schoolteacher and demand you apologise to her or anything," I said. "I guess your grandmother already did that."

"Yeah," she muttered. "She grounded me, and I had to stand here for hours while she dealt with all the people complaining about ghosts. She says it's a good learning experience for when I'm coven leader."

"Is that what you want?" I asked. "To lead the Meadowsweet Coven?"

She shrugged. "I dunno."

Tweens rarely had a handle on what they wanted out of life. I still didn't know now, really, at twenty-five. I'd just kind of muddled through life. My arrival at Fairy Falls was the first decision I'd made which had felt like I was moving in the right direction.

"Well, Alissa works at the hospital," I said. "She has healing magic. What type do you have?"

Sammi gave another shrug, fiddling with a loose thread on her cardigan. "I have the same. Healing magic. Most of my family does."

"You have time to decide," I added. "But try to think before you speak in the future, okay? Rebecca's been through a lot."

"Mm." Her gaze went to the desk, where a book lay open, titled *A Guide to Basic Rituals*. Madame Grey must have left it out. I gave the page a scan, but even the basics were far too advanced for me. Besides, there was no point in looking up how to use the sceptre when it was missing. A *Guide to Banishing Ghosts for Dummies* would be more helpful right now.

Or *talking* to ghosts. Like my mother. Raising the dead was illegal, but if they came back on their own, it was another story. Curiosity seized me, but before I could investigate the bookshelves behind the desk, Madame Grey re-entered the office.

"Sammi, you can go," she said.

Her granddaughter nodded and ducked out of the room.

Madame Grey closed the door behind her. "I do hope you haven't come to report a haunting, Blair. Your boss has left me fifteen messages."

"Oh, no," I said. "It sounds like our office isn't the worst case, if this is happening all over town. Is there nothing you can do?"

She walked to the desk and closed the ritual textbook. "Any of us can banish a single spirit using a spell, but this sort of epidemic can only be reversed by removing the cause."

My heart sank. "You mean, by finding the sceptre. Not by waiting until after Samhain."

"Yes, Blair," she said. "I take it you've thoroughly searched the house?"

"Alissa and I looked around the whole place yesterday," I said. "And nobody lied when they said they didn't kill Grace, unless I wasn't thorough enough with my questionings. But that's not what I wanted to talk to you about. Aveline confirmed what Nathan's dad said about— about my mum being a criminal. She said *Tanith* stole the sceptre, once. Is it true?"

Madame Grey's lips pressed into a thin line. "I knew the sceptre was stolen once before, but not who was responsible. Aveline never mentioned it to me, and nor did your grandmother. I wonder what possessed her to confide in you?"

Er... a werewolf potion. Which I'd forgotten about, thanks to the ghosts. "I don't know why she didn't tell anyone. How did nobody from Fairy Falls hear about it?"

Had anyone really known my mother at all?

"We only knew her as a child," she said. "She left the town when she was eighteen. At the time, she still carried a membership to the Wildflower Coven. Her only surviving family member was her mother... your grandmother. Her disappearance wasn't unusual, given her adventurous nature. She's not the first witch to leave town in search of excitement."

It sounds like she found more than excitement. "Aveline probably only knew because she was the sceptre's owner. But I don't understand why my mother would take it to begin with."

"If I know one thing about Tanith, it's that she rarely did things without reason."

"Aveline said she was prone to making rash decisions," I said. "I take it running away with a fairy isn't conventional?"

"No, but Tanith would never harm anyone. She had a very strong moral code."

I swallowed down bitter words. Maybe I was naïve in my continuing belief that there was an explanation for my mother's actions which didn't hinge on her being a career criminal, but it was either that or believe that maybe... maybe she'd never wanted me to begin with.

You were never supposed to be part of this world, Nathan's father had said. Madame Grey had unambiguously told me he was talking complete nonsense, and yet...

"If Aveline knows more about Tanith, she's never told me, Blair," said Madame Grey. "I didn't lie to you."

True. "Thanks for talking to me."

If anything, I felt even worse than I had before when I left her office. The road was still mired in thick fog, and since it got dark earlier at this time of year, it was all I could do not to trip over my own feet. When I reached the doorstep to the house, I *did* trip—over a small bundle of fur sprawled across the entryway.

"Whoa, Sky. Didn't see you there."

Usually at night, all I could see was his one white paw. In the fog, the only part of him still visible was his bright blue eye. His grey eye had merged with the fog, and the sight of a single disembodied cat's eye staring at me was pretty creepy.

"Are you hoping Aveline trips over you on the way out?" I asked. "Or—there aren't any ghosts in the house, are there?"

I checked my phone and found a new message from Alissa telling me she was going to be late back from work due to a ghost infestation at the hospital.

"I think I should go and help Alissa, right, Sky?"

Madame Grey's words had left me restless, and besides, being alone in the house with a potential murderer was unappealing enough even without any unwanted ghosts hanging around. Maybe I had seen my mother's spirit that morning, but now wasn't the time to go wandering around the hills in the dark. Finding my way to the high street was difficult enough, and I took three wrong turnings on the way to Alissa's workplace. Given the number of people walking into one another, it was a good job nobody in the town drove cars.

I stumbled my way into the hospital, colliding with Vincent the vampire in the doorway.

"Whoa." I jumped back, wincing when I hit my elbow on the door frame. "Sorry, didn't see you there. Were you —right, you were at the blood bank, right?"

"Yes," he said, looking disgruntled. "This ghost epidemic is very inconvenient."

"Vampires can see ghosts?" I asked.

"Most of us can," he said. "Our enhanced senses make navigating this perplexing fog easier, but not for everyone else."

"I guess not." I covered my ears as a ghostly howling struck up in the corridor to our right. "I should have known the hospital would be flooded with spirits. I take it they're all over your house, too?"

"Surprisingly not," he said. "Ghosts often return to places they lived in, and nobody actually *lives* in the morgue except for us."

"Never thought I'd envy you for sleeping in coffins," I said. "So the ghosts are just appearing in the places they used to live in?"

"Or where they died," he said. "But most bodies that show up at the morgue are already dead."

"I'd hope so, considering," I said. "So if I wanted to find a specific ghost..."

Wait a second. Never mind chasing my dead mother— Grace had died so recently that her spirit must be closer to this world than most of the others. What if it was possible to bring her back to reveal the identity of her murderer?

"Not thinking of dabbling in necromancy, are you?" he enquired.

"No, but I was thinking now's a good chance to question a murder victim," I replied.

"And your mother."

I stepped back. "I thought you weren't reading my mind anymore."

"Tread carefully around the dead," he said. "They might resemble their living selves, but they're not the same. They're not alive, and they have no wants or needs. Make no mistake, they should not be walking among the living."

"This coming from a vampire?" Maybe I should have kept that thought to myself—not that he couldn't have plucked it from my mind anyway.

"I was not raised from death by a magical force beyond comprehension as these spirits were," he said. "I would advise you to ask an expert witch or wizard if you wish to contact a specific spirit without inviting trouble into your house."

He disappeared, leaving me alone outside the hospital and wishing I'd asked Madame Grey about questioning Grace's ghost. Perhaps she already planned to, regardless of the magical world's usual feelings on summoning the dead.

Unless we found the sceptre, the town was doomed to be haunted no matter what. Why not take advantage of that to solve the murder?

———

I woke to an early morning call from Veronica saying the office was closed for the day because the printer and the coffee machine had got into a fight with the ghost in the middle of the night. Fervently glad not to be dealing with *that* mess, I tried to get back to sleep, but now I was awake, Aveline's words came crashing back into my head, along with the reminder that we had one less day to track down the sceptre. Small mercies that nobody seemed to have noticed the Head Witch's abrupt change in personality and no ghosts had appeared inside the house. Our house might be old, but it seemed nobody had died here… with one obvious exception.

Sky meowed and curled up under my arm, his tail tickling my nose. Fairy cat or not, he was downright affectionate when he wanted to be. "The ghosts don't bother you, do they? Can you see them?"

"Miaow." I winced when his claws dug into my chest, in a manner that implied that if I was awake, I'd better feed him. I fished in my bag for a treat and tossed it to him, and Sky settled down in the spot on Nina's sofa where I'd been lying.

All right. I guess I'm getting up, then.

Madame Grey was bound to be unimpressed if I asked her for a guide to summoning spirits, so the university library was a safer bet. I took a quick shower and dressed before heading downstairs to meet Alissa.

"Hey, Blair," she said, locking the door to her flat—*our* flat. "No work today?"

"The ghost wrecked our office," I said. "So I thought I'd take a trip over to the university library and see if they have any guidebooks on how I might contact Grace's ghost."

If we both had today free, then now was the perfect time to do some ghost-hunting.

"Good thinking," she said. "Aveline was pretty quiet last night, all things considered."

"No wonder, if she's had a double dose of that were-wolf potion."

"Speaking of the werewolf potion, I think someone threw it in the bin," she said. "Did I mention I'm sick of people making a mess of our flat?"

"Speak for yourself." I dug my hands in my pockets, shivering as we walked out into the fog. "Sunday can't come quickly enough."

"I can't believe my grandmother is organising another rehearsal this evening in this weather," said Alissa. "Half the town's shops are closed, and the hospital has had to move all the patients to the east wing because it's the only place that isn't haunted."

"Another rehearsal? You're joking." I groaned. "How does she expect anyone to see where they're going? And what if a dozen ghosts join the procession?"

"I told her that," said Alissa. "She insisted. It's not worth arguing with her when she's in one of her moods. Anyway, given that the werewolf potion is scheduled to wear off by tonight, we're best staying out of the Head Witch's way."

"Just what we need— Aveline back to her usual self." I led the way uphill towards the town's only university, which lay at the far end of town. "Wish we could exorcise *her*."

At this rate, Fairy Falls would need its own ghost extermination team. Most of the current security force couldn't see ghosts... including Nathan.

"Tell me about it," said Alissa. "It's quiet out here, considering half the town's off work. Is Nathan free? I'm guessing not, since you didn't invite him with us."

"No, he's still on security duty," I said. "I don't know

how he can see where he's going. Even the High Fliers aren't out in this weather."

"This might help." Alissa pulled out her wand and gave it a wave, conjuring up a spark of light to show the path through the fog.

"That's a useful one." I pulled out my own wand and did likewise. My torchlight was a little too much like a disco ball for my liking, but at least I could see more than a few inches in front of me. We made our way uphill to the university campus, where the fog masked the murals on the walls of the brick buildings.

"My mum used to teach here," Alissa said. "Before she left academia to work in the herb greenhouses. You've been here before… right, when you were looking into Dr Appleton's murder."

"Which turned out not to be a murder," I added. "Yeah, and I know someone in the library who might help me out."

It took a while to find the right building, not helped by the campus's confusing layout which was tricky to navigate even without ground-level fog. At least the inside of the library was fog-free, though there was no sign of Samuel the vampire either.

Alissa scanned the curving rows of shelves. "Where's your friend?"

"He's—" I paused as Samuel the vampire appeared out of nowhere on my right. The vampire had dark skin and short hair and wore his usual smart suit. I'd never seen a vampire who dressed sloppily. Presumably they covered it in vampire training. "Here," I finished.

"Blair Wilkes," he said. "I haven't seen you in a while."

"I've been busy," I said. "You wouldn't happen to have any books on ghosts, would you?"

"I'm afraid most of them have been taken out by the History Department. There's a particularly stubborn poltergeist wreaking havoc on the third floor."

"It's happening here, too?" asked Alissa.

He fixed his gaze on her. "I've never seen you before. Are you new?"

To my astonishment, Alissa blushed. "Ah, no, I'm not a student. I studied medicine, though, and I work at the hospital now. I'm Alissa."

"I'm Samuel," he said. "Is there another book I can help you find? Or perhaps you would like to come to the café for a drink instead?"

I cleared my throat. "We're not trying to banish a ghost," I said. "We're trying to summon one."

"Why didn't you say so?" His gaze was still on Alissa, his eyes unblinking in that odd vampire way. "I believe we have one or two left… anything else?"

"Anything on the sceptre?" I asked. "And Samhain, rituals… that type of thing?"

"Unfortunately, Madame Grey has all those," he said. "I heard rumours that the sceptre's disappearance was linked to the current epidemic."

"I think it's true," I said, with a glance at Alissa. "I know Madame Grey and the others have their own books, but I wondered if there was anything here that might help us attract a specific ghost. Not banish them."

"I will see." He vanished, leaving a blurred imprint on my eyelids. Yet another thing they must cover in vampire training. I'd never met a vampire who *didn't* move in that way.

"You didn't mention a vampire worked here," Alissa whispered.

"I thought I did," I said. "It's quiet in here. Maybe the library's ghost-proofed."

"Here," said Samuel, appearing in another flash with a book in his hands. "This is a basic guide which concerns summoning spirits. I rather think everyone wants to do the opposite, given the circumstances."

"So do we." I took the book from him. "But there's something else we need to do first."

His gaze went to Alissa. "Let me know if you change your mind. About going with me for coffee."

She blinked at him. "Ah. Sure."

I rolled my eyes and put the book into my bag. "C'mon. Let's go."

Alissa hesitated a moment, then followed me. "I didn't think vampires could even drink coffee."

"Flirting with vampires again?" I raised an eyebrow at her as we left the building. "I'm starting to think you have a type."

She poked me in the shoulder. "Oi. Just because you're immune to his charm…"

"Vampires aren't my type."

"No, that's Nathan," she said. "Speaking of whom— what's he doing?"

"Patrolling in the fog." I adjusted the bag with the book on my shoulder. "I need a warm drink before I head out there. And *not* with a vampire."

11

Inside Charms & Caffeine, we found what seemed like half the town's population, sheltering from the fog and the ghosts. Alissa and I bought coffee and muffins, snagging a table the instant one became available.

"New recipe from out of town, I heard." Alissa bit into her muffin. "I approve."

I took a bite and sighed in contentment as the taste of cinnamon flooded my mouth, instantly warming me from head to toe. "Let's read the book before we summon any spirits."

Alissa leaned forward as I placed the library book on the table. "The town has enough ghosts wandering around without us inviting more unwanted guests from beyond the grave."

"Definitely." I glanced around before opening the book in case anyone was snooping, but everyone else in the coffee shop was too busy discussing the ghost situation to notice us reading the instructions for a spirit-summoning spell. Alissa copied out the list of ingredients, and once we'd finished our coffees, we headed to the apothecary to buy what we needed.

"I'm surprised more people didn't have the same idea," Alissa remarked as we left with a bag full of herbs. "Considering how rare it is for ghosts to appear at all."

"Maybe they're too preoccupied dealing with the ghosts who are already here." If my dad's letter hadn't put the idea in my mind of talking to my mother, I'd never have considered using the spell at all, but who better to question about the murderer than the ghost of their victim?

Grace could be a test run, and then—only then—would I consider trying to contact Tanith Wildflower.

"Where do you want to do this?" I asked Alissa. "Grace died in our garden, but I dread to think what Aveline would do if she caught us summoning ghosts. Not to mention if the killer's inside the house, they might try to bump *us* off next."

Alissa's lips pursed. "You're right. Given the state of the town, it shouldn't matter where we do the summoning, so we should pick somewhere nobody's likely to walk in on us."

"In the woods, then?" I suggested.

"By the lake would be better," she said. "The woods are full of confused werewolves and elves getting lost in the fog."

I used my wand to cast another light spell to illuminate the path to the lake. "Most people don't seem to be panicking, do they? They can't all have guessed this is happening because of the sceptre."

"No, but it's Samhain." Alissa adjusted her grip on the

bag of ingredients. "Besides, if the whole town shut down every time some magical catastrophe happened, we'd never get anything done."

"Fair point. It'll be over soon, anyway." Once we found the sceptre, that is.

We reached the path that ran parallel to the lake. The 'Welcome to Fairy Falls' sign looked even more sinister than usual, lurking crookedly in the fog.

"We should stop here." Alissa came to a halt. "If we go any further, we might walk *into* the lake."

"I don't fancy a swim in this weather." I shivered. "What do the merpeople think of all this?"

"They're probably hiding further away from shore. I don't think the ghosts are haunting anywhere outside the town, so they'll be keeping their distance."

She seemed to be right. The lake appeared deserted, and I found a clear spot of grass on the bank, near the path up into the hills where the Samhain ceremony was set to take place. The wind howled through the fog as we carefully laid out the ingredients according to the instructions in the book.

Alissa faced the circle of herbs we'd assembled. "Grace Rosemary, we wish to speak with you."

Silence, aside from the howl of the wind and the faint crash of the waterfall.

"Maybe we should have avoided the lake," I said through chattering teeth. "Her ghost might try to drown us for all we know."

"Relax." Alissa moved closer to me. "The ghosts aren't any creepier than anything else you've seen in the paranormal world, and they can't harm you."

"The pirate ghost wasn't too bad," I allowed. "Where is she?"

"Grace?" Alissa called out, turning on the spot. "Maybe she's already somewhere else in town."

I squinted into the fog in search of a figure with pink hair. Blurred shapes filled the whiteness, and I was sure one further up the hillside looked human-like. "Hello?"

No reply. I took a step uphill and tripped over, dropping my wand on the grass.

"There's nobody there, I don't think," said Alissa. "Not Grace, anyway. We'd know it was her by the hair."

I crouched to look for my wand. "I thought I saw someone, but maybe not."

It's not her. The figure was so indistinct, there was nothing to prove it might be my mother other than my own overactive imagination. Besides, Tanith Wildflower wouldn't appear without speaking to me, right?

I found my wand and picked it up, relighting the spell to illuminate the hillside. At my feet were the scattered remains of old herbs, not part of our spell circle. Had someone else tried a summoning on this very spot?

Alissa's phone buzzed. "Ah—it's my grandmother. Oh—what? No, we didn't. Why, who took it?"

"Took what?" I mouthed at her.

Alissa covered the phone with her hand. "Someone broke into Madame Grey's office."

My heart sank into my shoes. "The same thief as before? What did they take this time?"

"One of her books." Alissa spoke into the phone again. "Yes, Blair's with me... all right. Okay. Fine." She hung up. "She's insisting on the rehearsal being moved up to midday, since the academy teachers can't keep their students under control with ghosts in all the classrooms."

"She just got robbed and she's still fixated on rehearsing for the ceremony?" I said in disbelief. "Why?"

"Because she plans to have a team of witches search the whole town while everyone else is up in the hills," she explained. "The other witches from out of town will be participating, too."

"Including Aveline?" Uh-oh. What if she was still under the effects of the werewolf potion? Granted, it would be an improvement, but we should be looking for the thief and the murderer, not rehearsing for a ceremony which might not happen at all, the way things were going.

"I don't know," said Alissa. "But the book the thief stole was a guide to rituals involving the sceptre. Perhaps she thinks the ceremony will bring the thief out of hiding. Whoever they are, they won't stand a chance against the combined strength of all the town's witches and wizards."

"I saw that book on her desk." I frowned. "So our thief wasn't an expert on the sceptre, then?"

"Doesn't look like it." She pocketed her phone. "Unless they're planning to claim the sceptre on Samhain and want to make sure it chooses them."

"Is that even possible?" A knot of dread formed inside my chest.

"There are ways... dark magic rituals they might use to ensure they're picked, if they're unscrupulous enough." Her mouth pinched with distaste. "I hope it won't come to that. My grandmother, though... she's worried."

She had reason to be. If we failed to get the sceptre back today, there was nothing to stop the thief from claiming the title of Head Witch.

———

The rehearsal went as well as one might have expected, considering the fog, the marshy ground, and the ghosts. If Madame Grey intended to draw out the thief, they could have followed the back of the procession all the way to the lake and nobody would have noticed.

Sky not only refused to wear his pointy hat, he swiped viciously at my ankle when I tried to put it on his head. In fairness, he wasn't the only familiar misbehaving. The owl familiars kept flying into one another in the low lighting, several cats started fights with one another, and every few minutes, a ghost would pass through the line and leave a trail of pandemonium behind. It was no wonder it took me several minutes to hear Madame Grey's voice shouting at the front.

"Aveline—stop! Stop that at once!"

There was a flash of light. I ran out of the line towards it, ignoring Alissa's shout of warning. What was the Head Witch doing this time?

Another flash of light, this one closer. Aveline stood in front of the procession, which had drawn to a halt. For a heartbeat, I thought she held the sceptre, but it was just her borrowed walking stick. In her other hand, she pointed her wand at the terrified-looking academy students.

"If you failed to find the thief, it must be because they're among us right now," she said to Madame Grey. "This ought to scare them out of hiding."

She waved her wand, and the students scattered. Madame Grey raised her own wand, and a collective gasp rose from among the assembled witches and wizards as she turned it on the Head Witch. "Calm yourself, Aveline. You're not thinking clearly."

I glanced behind me, but I'd left Alissa in the fog, behind a swarm of students, all of whom were watching with frightened eyes.

Aveline waved her wand again—and stopped mid-wave, her entire body frozen on the spot. Gradually, a look of calm came over her, and she lowered her hands.

Madame Grey's mouth flattened into a thin line. "Rebecca, what have I told you about using your powers?"

Another audible gasp came from the students. *Whoa. Rebecca's powers even worked on the Head Witch?*

Rebecca looked defiantly at Madame Grey, her hands fisted at her sides. "I had to do something. She was going to attack us."

"Go," Madame Grey said, gesturing to the students. "Go and find your teachers. Rebecca, come here."

"I can undo it." Rebecca hurried forwards out of the group, her head bowed.

Sammi said in a carrying whisper, "I knew she was a freak."

Holding Toast tightly to her chest, Rebecca burst into sobs. "I wanted to help," she gasped. "I'm sorry."

"Rebecca, we've talked about this," said Madame Grey, in disappointed tones. "I thought you knew better. You overpowered the Head Witch in front of an audience, with a thief in town and someone using our tools for ill."

Her face paled. "I—I didn't think."

"You weren't the only one." Madame Grey paced around Aveline. "She's under the effects of another spell, too."

I clapped my hands to my mouth. "Oh, no. It's my fault—I'm the one who gave her the potion."

"You gave her a potion that causes agitation and confusion?" said Madame Grey.

"No, a werewolf potion. Why, did someone else…?" I trailed off. "The potion should have worn off by now."

"Blair, take Alissa and go home," she said. "Search the house before the others get there. Fast."

My throat went dry. "What about the ceremony tomorrow—is it going ahead either way?"

"Yes," she said. "It is."

Tomorrow. Unless a miracle showed up, there would be no sceptre at the procession this Samhain.

I ran back to Alissa and our familiars, slipping in the mud and skidding to a halt at her side.

"We need to go," I said in an undertone. "Madame Grey thinks Aveline was under some kind of spell that causes agitation and confusion, and we're to search the house before she gets back."

Alissa's eyes widened. "Was it a spell? Are you sure?"

"It can't be the werewolf potion." I beckoned Sky to follow me, and he did. He had no problem obeying my commands out of the context of wearing a pointed hat. "The potion doesn't have any side-effects, and it should have worn off by now anyway. I guess someone else had a similar idea."

While I understood Madame Grey's concern, I hoped she'd go easy on Rebecca. She'd only been trying to help her fellow students.

The house was silent when Alissa and I got home. Sky padded through the door and headed upstairs without looking back.

"Guess I was lucky he showed up for the rehearsal today at all," I remarked.

"Hmm." Alissa unlocked the door to our flat. "Agitation and confusion sounds like a potion, but you'd think Aveline would be careful before drinking any strange concoctions."

"Unless she was still under the effects of the werewolf potion and wasn't cautious enough?" I swallowed, guilt churning inside me.

Alissa shook her head. "My grandmother told me Vanessa prepares all the Head Witch's food and drink. When she doesn't, she uses spells to test everything for poisons."

"So might *Vanessa* have done it?" It would explain why she hadn't killed Aveline outright. She didn't want her dead, she just wanted her position as Head Witch.

Alissa and I searched the inside of our flat, finding no empty mugs or cups with traces of an unknown potion. Or stolen books of ritual magic, come to that. Not that I expected the thief would leave it out in the open, considering nobody had seen so much as a glimpse of the sceptre since its disappearance.

"Better check the other flat before the others get back." I made for the door facing ours. The room within was as tidy as the last time I'd seen it. No sign of anything out of place. "I wish I'd got a closer look at the textbook's cover, so I'd recognise it if I saw it."

"I doubt they'd have left it out in the open." Alissa walked around the living room. "They must suspect we've searched the house when nobody's around."

I entered the room Vanessa slept in, halting beside her half-open suitcase. No books, but an odd smell hung around her folded clothes. I carefully lifted a layer of shirts aside and found a small bag that smelled distinctly of herbs at the bottom.

"Potion making ingredients." Alissa leaned over my shoulder. "What type did my grandmother think was used on Aveline?"

"Something for agitation and confusion." I placed the folded shirts back into position. "I don't know what Vanessa would have to gain by using a potion on her mother if she *didn't* steal the sceptre."

Leaving the suitcase as I'd found it, I went to search Shannon's room next. The small bedroom contained even less than Vanessa's room, and her open suitcase revealed no hidden surprises.

That just left the flat upstairs. Alissa led the way, and I tensed at every creak in the floorboards.

"I don't trust any of those witches," she said, pushing on the door to the upstairs flat and finding it locked. "The twins weren't even at the rehearsal, did you see?"

"Well, their mother did just die."

Alissa pulled out her wand to use an unlocking spell. The door sprang open, revealing a surprisingly empty room. Even the twins' suitcases were gone.

"Did they leave town?" Alissa strode into the room. "No… they can't have. Someone would have seen them."

"In that fog?" I scanned the plain furniture, the clean carpets. "Maybe the ghosts were the last straw. Or—or perhaps they thought they might be able to talk to Grace."

"If anything, that would give them more of an incentive to stick around," Alissa said. "I thought they'd want to find the killer before leaving."

"Me too."

Alissa trod across the living room, and I followed, peering into the bedroom. Traces of pink dye lay on the pillow, which smelled of oil and carpet cleaner, as usual, while an empty bottle lay on the floor.

Alissa wrinkled her nose. "She certainly left her mark on the walls of our shower. Nothing else in here, though. Maybe the twins used the potion on Aveline before they left town."

"Maybe," I said, but I had my doubts. Given the twins' livid reaction to their mother's passing, their disappearance made no sense. Had they managed to talk to Grace's ghost among the dead, and was that why she hadn't answered our call? It seemed unlikely, but why leave before justice was delivered?

My phone buzzed. "Hi, Nathan."

"Hey, Blair," he said. "I'm assuming you have the rest of the day free, so I'd like to take you out. Does that sound good to you?"

"Yeah, it really does." It would be the one bright spark in the crappiest week ever. Okay, except perhaps for my stint in jail. And the times I'd been targeted by a murderer. Still.

I did my best to shove all thoughts of murderers and missing sceptres from my mind as I got ready for my date with Nathan, but seeing him waiting on the doorstep for me brought my brain to a screeching halt. He looked particularly handsome tonight, wearing a shirt and jeans instead of his usual hunter-style getup. Until now, it hadn't hit me how much I'd missed him this week.

"Off duty?" I leaned in to kiss him.

"Until tomorrow morning." He took my hand and we walked to the pub, while I recounted the latest string of disasters, from the missing book to the failed rehearsal, Aveline's erratic behaviour and the twins' abrupt departure.

Nathan let out a low whistle when I'd finished. "Well, it's safe to say Madame Grey doesn't think the police have any expertise in this case. They haven't told us to get involved, anyway."

"Maybe because the sceptre isn't like a typical magical item." I walked into the pub, finding it as crowded as the coffee shop, most tables taken by people keen to avoid stepping outside in the fog. "And because Steve and most of the security team can't see ghosts."

"You can't see any in here, can you?"

I scanned the warm, bright pub. "No. That must be why it's so crowded."

"Our usual table is free." He took a seat, giving me a smile. "So—what happened with the Head Witch? Still being unbearable?"

"Well, she's improved, but only because I used a were-wolf potion on her and accidentally got the dose too high," I admitted. "But her behaviour today, flinging accusations at the students—I think the twins used a spell on her before they left as a farewell gift."

"The twins left town?" His brow furrowed. "Are you sure?"

"Yeah, so it seems," I said. "Something's odd about the whole situation, but everyone in town already has their hands full, especially Madame Grey."

"Perhaps they wanted to take their mother home to have a proper funeral, and intend to return later when the ghosts are gone," he said. "Any new leads on the thief?"

"Someone who doesn't know how to use the sceptre,

judging by the book they stole from Madame Grey's office." I tapped the menu to order food and drink. "Unless they were waiting until tomorrow."

"They might well be," he said. "I don't know how the witches plan on doing the ceremony in this weather, sceptre or none. The gargoyles can't even fly on patrol without crashing into one another."

I grinned. "Please tell me Steve did that."

"No, but two others got into a collision, including the guy with permanent ink stains on his face from that printer in your office."

I laughed aloud. "Speaking of printers, it got into a fight with a ghost last night."

"Which ghost again?"

"I didn't tell you about the ghost in the office?" I picked up my fork as our food appeared on the table. "It really has been a long week."

Being with Nathan always made me feel better, and the ghost in the office yesterday seemed more amusing than irritating when I repeated the story to him.

"Luckily, most people seem thrilled to have a three-day weekend," Nathan commented. "That might change if the ghosts are still here on Monday."

"Hope not." I stabbed a piece of pasta with my fork. "The fog is bad enough. If not for these boots, I'd have face-planted a dozen times on my way here."

"It's like that everywhere," he said. "We've had to employ vampires and shifters to patrol the woods without risk of injury."

"If it means you don't have to risk breaking your neck, then that's good with me," I said.

He smiled. "My eyesight isn't that bad, but I'll take any

excuse to get out of night-time patrols. I've spent entirely too little time with you this week."

I smiled. "It's appreciated, considering how busy you are."

"You're not still sleeping on Nina's sofa, are you?" he asked.

"It's that or my own sofa, next to Aveline's snoring." I shuddered.

"There's another option," he said. "My place, for instance."

My heart missed a beat. "You're not on the night shift?"

"No." He put down his beer glass. "It's up to you."

"Yes. I mean, I'd rather sleep in a pigsty than next to Aveline. Not that I'm implying your house is a pigsty…"

Why could I never get through a serious conversation without getting tongue-tied? Nathan and I were serious. Staying over at his house shouldn't be that big a deal.

"It's that or I stand outside your door all night," he said. "I wanted to last night, but I was on double security duty. I worried about you, considering everything that happened."

My mood sobered a little. "You think the killer's going to come back? We're down two suspects—three, counting Aveline."

"Whatever the killer's aim is, they're not done yet."

No kidding. And we'd find out before Samhain was over, one way or another. If I could forget it all, just for one night, I might have the strength to see tomorrow through.

12

I woke up on Samhain in the best mood I'd been in all week, which improved tenfold when I opened my eyes to the smell of delicious coffee.

"You're amazing." I accepted the mug from Nathan, my eyes half-closed. "Thought you had an early shift."

"I do," he said. "You can go back to sleep if you like."

Sky prodded me in the side and then climbed onto my lap, and I held the mug high to avoid spilling coffee everywhere. "Miaow."

"Good morning to you, too." I scratched him behind his ears with my free hand. "I didn't hear him come in."

"He wandered in here an hour ago and fell asleep on my head."

"Ah." I sipped my coffee. "I take it you're going to be patrolling at the ceremony?"

"Assuming it goes ahead, yes." He opened the curtains, which showed that the day was as foggy as the previous one. At least it wasn't raining.

ELLE ADAMS

I put my coffee down on the bedside table as my phone buzzed.

"Expecting a call?" Nathan asked.

"No…" I picked it up. "Alissa?"

"Blair." Her voice was breathless. "You'd better come back home now."

"Why? Is someone else dead?"

Her silence went on a second too long. I jumped upright, knocking my coffee mug flying.

"Don't worry about it," Nathan said to my hastened apologies. "Go on, see what she wants. Please be careful out there."

I threw my clothes on and left Sky sleeping, figured he deserved a nap before the ceremony. My feet hardly touched the ground as I flew home in a breathless sprint.

Alissa waited in the hall. "Blair, it's Shannon. I think she's dead."

"Oh, no." My gaze immediately went to our flat. "Does Aveline know?"

"I haven't dared wake her yet," she admitted. "I called my grandmother, but I wanted to know if you could see anything here that shouldn't be."

"Come quickly," Nina's faint voice came from upstairs. "The smell is making me nauseous."

I frowned. "That's not Shannon's room."

Alissa took the stairs two at a time. "I know. Hurry, before the others wake up."

I followed Alissa upstairs and found Nina waiting at the top. Without a word, she pushed open the door into the Rosemary witches' room.

Shannon's body lay sprawled in the room's centre, flat on her face, a bloody wound on the back of her head.

I clapped a hand to my mouth. "Who did this?"

"Whoever they were, they crept up on her from behind," Alissa said. "See anything?"

I dragged my gaze from Shannon's limp body and scanned the room. "No. When did you find her?"

"Five minutes before I called you. Nina found her first."

Nina edged into the room, her face ashen. "I heard footsteps on the stairs about twenty minutes before I found the body, but I was half asleep at the time. If I'd come sooner…"

"It's not your fault," I said. "What was Shannon even doing in here? The twins have left."

"Maybe she wanted their room," said Alissa doubtfully. "I called my grandmother, but she's stressed enough about the ceremony without us piling this on her."

"What was the murder weapon?" asked Nina. "It looks like she got hit with a heavy object."

"The sceptre?" I averted my gaze, feeling sick. "Why not use the same spell they used on Grace?"

"Haven't a clue." Alissa's mouth pinched. "I'm going to call the police. I know the last thing we need is Steve in our house—unless Nathan's free?"

"No, he's on duty." I looked around the room again in case I'd missed anything, but saw nothing out of place aside from Shannon's body. But what had Shannon been doing in here? It wasn't even her room. "Were they trying to take out the competition before the ceremony?"

"Speaking of which," Nina said. "How is Madame Grey supposed to go ahead with the ceremony with nearly all the Head Witch hopefuls dead or missing, and no sceptre?"

"Exactly," I said. "Alissa, has Aveline been asleep all night? Did you hear anything from her room?"

"I used an earplug charm, but she can't climb the stairs without help," she answered. "She's not under any kind of spell or potion—I checked."

Right... the spell for agitation and confusion. We never figured out who did that either.

"She's back to her friendly self, then?" I said.

"Yep," said Nina. "You should be glad you weren't here. She and Vanessa got into an argument over the Rosemary witches."

"Does Madame Grey seem bothered that they're gone?" I asked.

Alissa looked up from her phone. "You think *they* came back and killed her?"

"Maybe it was a cover." I was grasping at straws now. "I don't know, I'm making it up as I go along now. I'm tired."

"Busy night with Nathan," she said, with a grin.

Heat rose to my cheeks, and I elbowed her in the ribs. "Oi. Cut it out."

"You shouldn't have teased me about Samuel."

"Who?" said Nina.

"Her vampire 'friend'."

Alissa coughed. "We flirted for about four seconds. Hardly life partner material."

"You never know. Nathan and I met when he almost arrested me for trespassing." I jumped at the sound of a door opening downstairs. "Is that the police?"

Aveline's voice drifted upstairs. "What are you lot shouting about?"

"Shannon's dead," I told her. "The police are on their way to question everyone, so I'd suggest you get ready."

I didn't wait for a reply. I ran downstairs and was halfway down the hall when the door to my flat blew open and Aveline marched out, still wearing her flowery dressing gown. "Thought it was funny to take an old woman's walking stick, did you?"

"What's the problem this time?" I had no patience whatsoever for her drama when someone sneaked in here while I'd been gone—where my friends were sleeping— and committed murder. Ignoring the Head Witch, I banged on the door to the other flat.

Vanessa emerged, looking bewildered. "What is going on?"

"I can't find my walking stick!" yelled Aveline.

Perhaps it was the expression of careful surprise on Vanessa's face, or the way she reacted a second too late, but a sudden suspicion slammed into me.

"Back in a second." I hurried upstairs, nearly colliding with Alissa coming the opposite way.

"Whoa!" She caught herself against the wall. "What is it, Blair?"

"Aveline's walking stick is missing." I swallowed hard. "Shannon was killed by a heavy blow to the back of the head."

Alissa's eyes widened. "You don't think…?"

"I don't want to sound paranoid, but…" I ran the rest of the way upstairs and into the Rosemary witches' room, giving Shannon's body a wide berth. The bathroom door was slightly open. I gave it a quick push, then recoiled.

A bloody stick lay in the shower, bent at one end.

Alissa gasped behind me. Then downstairs, the door crashed open. "My grandmother's here. We're upstairs!"

There came the sound of footsteps on the stairs. I stepped back into the living room, averting my gaze from poor Shannon's inert body.

"The murder weapon is in the bathroom." Alissa moved aside to let her grandmother into the room.

Madame Grey walked past, peering through the open door. "The killer left it behind?"

"Perhaps they wanted to pin the blame on the Head Witch," I said. "She couldn't have climbed the stairs without help, though—we all know that."

"Indeed," Madame Grey said. "I will have to confiscate this and find another walking stick for Aveline. Meanwhile, we'll leave this room untouched for the police to examine."

"You'd think Vanessa would have brought a spare walking stick." I left the room, not sorry to leave the sight of Shannon's body behind. "There are only two possible suspects left, one of whom can't climb stairs."

Unless the Rosemary witches weren't as gone as they'd seemed... but why come back just to murder Shannon?

Alissa and I went downstairs and found Vanessa searching our living room, moving cushions around.

"There's no need for that," I said. "We've already found it."

"Found what?" Vanessa asked.

"Her walking stick," replied Alissa. "And the murder weapon."

Vanessa's face went white. "What are you saying?"

"Someone used Aveline's borrowed walking stick to kill Shannon," I said. "Odd choice for a weapon, isn't it?"

"I didn't!" she squeaked. "I told you, I wanted to win the leadership fair and square—"

"Where is the sceptre?" Madame Grey thundered from behind her. "Where did you put it?"

"I didn't take the sceptre!" she gasped. "I didn't lie—she knows. Blair knows."

She grabbed my arm, looking up at me imploringly. *She's not lying.*

I yanked my sleeve out of her grip. "She's telling the truth—at least at the moment, anyway. Did you kill Grace?"

"No!"

True.

Madame Grey's eyes narrowed. "I will examine the body. The house will remain under quarantine, and I will use detection spells on the walking stick to determine who carried it. If you want to make a confession, now is the time. That goes for all of you."

"There's an easier way," I said. "We summon Shannon's ghost."

A heartbeat passed. "I know about your little escapade yesterday, Blair," she said. "Alissa told me it didn't work."

Vanessa looked curiously between us. "What didn't work?"

"I still have some spare ingredients," Alissa said. "Let's try it on Shannon. It can't hurt."

Vanessa sank into an armchair. "I know what it looks like, but I'm not the killer. I knew we should have left as soon as the sceptre was taken."

Well, if it wasn't you, then it was Aveline herself. She wasn't faking her inability to climb stairs, though, unless the two of them had worked together. Or perhaps she'd bullied Vanessa into conspiring with her.

One way to find out.

The others watched in silence as Alissa and I set up the same arrangement of herbs as we'd used in the field. While summoning a ghost into my flat wasn't my idea of a good time, the only way to know the truth was to speak to the woman herself… and hope that her ghost was more talkative than Grace's was.

"Shannon," I whispered. "Can you hear me?"

Silence.

"Shannon." I spoke louder, and Alissa spoke, too.

"Shannon Grover," Madame Grey said, adding her voice to the chorus.

The herbs stirred on the spot as though caught in a breeze from an open window. Then the air shimmered, and a transparent figure appeared in mid-air. Seconds passed and the face of the floating figure became more distinct, resolving into Shannon herself.

Hey, it worked!

Shannon looked down at me. "Blair? What are you doing here? What am *I* doing here?"

"You died," said Alissa. "Who killed you?"

Her face fell. "I didn't see," she whispered. "I heard voices upstairs, so I went to look. And they sneaked up on me from behind."

"You didn't see who it was?" I asked.

"I don't know," she whispered. "Everything went black, and I was floating. The next thing I knew, I was… gone."

True. As far as I could tell. "Was Aveline or Vanessa there?"

"I don't know!" She pressed her hands to her ears, her expression distraught. "I can't hear myself think."

There was a loud knock on the door. Madame Grey rose to her feet from the sofa. "That'll be Steve."

"Oh, great."

The door opened and the gargoyle policeman walked in. "How did I know you'd be at the centre of this, Blair?"

"Who are you?" squeaked Shannon's ghost.

Steve looked straight through her. "Well? Have nothing to say for yourself, do you?"

"Blair wasn't even here," Alissa said. "Also, we're speaking to a ghost, but I'm guessing you can't see her."

"I really am dead?" Shannon sank on the spot in a dead faint.

Alissa and I looked at one another. "Since when could ghosts pass out?" I said.

Steve made a growling noise. "Enough of this nonsense. Tell me what happened here."

13

Steve, as usual, was of no help whatsoever. He questioned Vanessa intently and tried the same on Aveline until she attempted to curse him, at which point Vanessa had collapsed into hysterics.

The Head Witch was now at the top of my suspect list, but why would she steal her own sceptre? Or kill Shannon, come to that? Once the questioning was over, she'd gone to sulk inside my flat, refusing to let anyone else speak with her. She seemed not to remember anything of her time under the influence of the werewolf potion—that, or she was too stubborn to mention it.

Whoever the thief was, the sceptre's power would be at its peak tonight. That meant the person who'd stolen it might well be able to access more of its powers. Once Steve finished the questioning, I went outside to get some air. Ghostly forms occasionally drifted past, but none stopped to chat. I still had some of the ingredients for the ghost-summoning spell in my bag, and for the lack of anything better to do, I found myself wandering in the direction of the town cemetery. It was the obvious place to look for a ghost, but Tanith Wildflower wasn't even buried here. She couldn't be, if nobody in town had known she was dead. I didn't know where my mother had lived when she'd been alive, but maybe Vincent did. I hesitated, then knocked on the door to the house next to the cemetery.

It took several minutes before Vincent answered the door, a scowl on his face. Oops. I'd interrupted his nap. "What are you doing here, Blair?"

"You wouldn't happen to know where my mother lived when she was alive, would you?"

His frown deepened. "I thought I told you to be careful with the dead."

"I am, but today is my last chance." I glanced at the foggy cemetery. It looked even more eerie than usual, but then again, so did the whole town. "Is there a memorial or anything in there?"

"I imagine there is," he said. "I thought you were after a thief and a killer."

"We hit a dead end. Well, a ghostly one. She didn't see her killer. And the other ghost refused to show up. Please, Vincent. It's a one-off."

"*Mortals.*" He really did look tired. "You spend your whole lives pining for those who you have lost. Fine, go ahead and summon your ghost."

"Hey, I only found out my mother was dead a couple of months ago," I said indignantly. "There aren't any zombies or poltergeists or anything on the loose in there, are there?"

"Not that I know of."

And he was gone, the door closing behind him. My gaze darted to the iron gates to the cemetery, which was surrounded by high fences. My skin prickled. Maybe this wasn't such a great idea, but if I passed up the chance to talk to my mother like I had with my dad on the solstice, I knew I'd regret it forever.

The cemetery was much fancier than I'd expected, with neat rows of elaborately designed headstones. Every few feet stood a plaque telling me which coven the graves' occupants belonged to. It looked like all the witches and wizards were buried in clusters according to their coven or family.

Since there weren't any surviving members of my mother's coven, I started at the beginning of the first row. As I got further into the cemetery, the headstones' designs became more and more extravagant until they left a wide space around a tomb engraved with the Grey family name. Madame Grey's and Alissa's relatives had a whole mausoleum to themselves. It made sense, considering they owned the whole town.

A clattering sounded nearby, and my heart gave a violent jolt. *Calm down. Even if it's a ghost, they can't hurt you.*

Doing my best to ignore the prickle of unease on the back of my neck, I kept walking, past the stone building to the next segment of headstones.

The name *Wildflower* leapt out at me, drawing me to a halt. A small collection of graves, old and not well-kept, bore the name of my mother's coven. Nobody came here and left flowers like they did the others. The text on the front grave was cracked, the graves overgrown with weeds. Tears stung my eyes and I made a mental note to stop by here more often.

None of the graves was marked with Tanith's name, but I hadn't expected to find it. She'd died elsewhere, after all. With trembling hands, I pulled out the remaining herbs from my bag.

"What are you doing, girl?" a voice said from somewhere in the fog.

I dropped the herbs, backing away from the figure who'd appeared floating over another row of graves not far from the Wildflowers. She was so faded that all I could tell was that she wore a dress and had long curly hair.

"Did you come here to disturb the dead?" She gave the herbs a disapproving look. "We're disturbed enough by this disruption as it is."

"Have you seen the ghost of Tanith Wildflower?" I asked. "That's who I came to see."

"Who? Oh, that one." Her gaze went to the gravestones beside me. "No, because she wasn't buried here."

"Where was she buried, then?" I didn't expect an answer from a strange ghost I didn't know, but something compelled me to go on. The grave the new spirit had appeared above was so unkempt and overgrown, I couldn't even read the name on it.

"They took her, didn't they?" she said quietly.

"They?" I echoed. "Who?"

The spirit faded away, leaving nothing behind but the grave. I moved to the spot where she'd vanished, trying to make out the name on the stone. *She knew my mother... but who took her? The hunters?*

I picked up the herbs I'd dropped and rubbed my chilly hands together to warm them. Drops of dew from the weeds clung to my hands, along with... glitter. I glanced down and saw a thin trail of purple leading among the headstones.

"Is someone else here?" I walked down the row of graves. The glittery trail grew thicker as I approached the massive tomb that belonged to the Grey family.

What's a fairy doing here?

Wait... my dad had implied that the fairies were supposed to be more active on Samhain. Like the ghosts. That didn't give them a reason to hang around a cemetery, unless...

"Hey," I called. "Pixie. Is that you?"

He appeared in a flash of purple light, making alarmed chittering noises.

"What are you doing here?" I stepped towards him.

He flew down and into my face, forcing me to stumble backwards. His tiny hands pushed at me, his hands flailing, his mouth making noises I couldn't understand.

"What are you doing near Alissa's family's tomb?"

Ignoring him, I approached the mausoleum. It was certainly fancy-looking, with engraved artwork all over the exterior. The smell of fresh flowers hung around the place.

I took the heavy door handle and pushed inwards.

My instincts were right: the tomb wasn't empty at all. A short figure stood on the stone tiles, and she held the sceptre.

Sammi turned around, saw me, and let out a shriek, dropping the sceptre. "You promised nobody would disturb me!"

"You did it?" I looked at the pixie. "Since when were you friends with Sammi?"

And since when had she had reason to be a thief? Let alone murder—no, she couldn't have killed Grace or Shannon. Something more was going on here.

The pixie didn't answer, but he flew towards her, avoiding my gaze. He'd been with Sammi all along? Even when he'd delivered my dad's message?

"You let her steal the sceptre?" I said to him. "Or—no, you took it for her, didn't you? You used your glamour to hide and fly it out of the house right in front of the Head Witch."

She, unlike me, couldn't see through glamour. I'd taken the glitter I'd found in the bedroom and on the windowsill to be my own, but it wasn't. The pixie had already been in the flat, knowing I'd never suspect him of stealing from me after all he'd done to help me keep in contact with my dad.

The pixie fluttered in agitated circles, his tiny face flushed with shame. Sammi stood defensively in front of him. "He was trying to help me."

"This is the same pixie who once tried to 'help' me by crashing a dinner party at my boyfriend's house and throwing glitter everywhere," I said. "I thought you didn't like fairies."

"I didn't say that." She scrambled to pick up the sceptre. "I'm going to give it back as soon as I'm done, I swear. I didn't mean for all this to happen."

"Two people are dead," I said. "The Samhain ceremony is tonight, and your grandmother is under intense pressure trying to figure out how to do it without the sceptre. Not to mention the ghosts. You did that, didn't you?"

"I wanted to raise her. My mother." She swallowed.

"But it didn't work. I followed the instructions and the veil opened and all these ghosts came out, but not her."

"So you stole the book, too," I guessed. "To see if it could tell you what you did wrong."

She hung her head. "I wanted to undo it, but my magic isn't powerful enough."

"Well—look, do you have the book with you?" As annoyed as I was with her, she was still just a kid. Look at all the mistakes Rebecca had made. "Maybe we can both figure it out."

She shook her head. "It's too late. I don't think the ghosts will go away until after Samhain is over. I can't make it stop…"

"Maybe Aveline can," I said. "Since she's still its owner —until tonight, anyway. We should go and hand it back to her."

If she was willing to listen at all. Unless she'd killed Shannon or Grace…

"My grandmother is going to ground me for a lifetime." Her eyes brimmed over. "I just wanted to see my mum. I don't understand what the fuss is about. This is the time of year when spirits from the other side are active in this world anyway."

"Yes, but that's not what the sceptre is for," I said. "I wanted to do the same, you know—summon the ghost of my mother. But life and death… it's not for us to control.'

She rubbed her eyes with one hand. "Then what do I do?"

"Hand the sceptre to me, and I'll take it along to the ceremony so the new Head Witch can be chosen."

Sammi swallowed hard, then she extended a hand, the sceptre glowing under the dim ceiling lights of the tomb.

My hand closed around its base, and footsteps came from behind me.

"I'm afraid I can't let you do that," said a voice.

Grace stood in the entryway to the tomb, very much alive. On either side of her stood one of the twins—and all three of them pointed their wands at us.

14

For an instant, Sammi and I stood frozen, the sceptre suspended between us. Then I secured my grip and turned to face the three newcomers. Grace's bright pink hair was unmistakable, while the twins wore identical grins as though pleased with themselves for their deception.

"Give me that," said Grace. "You have no idea what you're doing with it, either of you."

Sammi looked from me to them, confused. "Are they with you?"

"Definitely not." My grip tightened around the sceptre's base. "How did you know we were in here?"

I darted a look at Sammi, wishing there was another way out of the tomb so she could make a run for safety. But there was only the front door, and the three other witches blocked the way. I wouldn't put her in the path of harm if I could help it.

"Lucky guess," said Grace. "You've led us on a wild ride, girl. Clever of you to keep the sceptre hidden in your room. I doubt your grandmother ever thought of looking there."

"I didn't do it to help you." Sammi was shaking. "I'm not trying to hurt anyone. I just wanted to bring back my mother from the dead—"

"Oh, that?" said Grace. "That's the least of what you can do with that sceptre. I'm more than happy to give a demonstration."

I looked between them. "So you figured out she stole it and thought you'd take it for yourself, did you? And you faked your own death so nobody would suspect you?"

"At least one of you has some intelligence," muttered Grace. "It's a waste. Give the sceptre over to us and I'll spare your life. You can't handle three of us at once."

Sammi made a choked noise. "You're murderers. I won't help you."

I gripped the sceptre, wishing I knew how to use it without risking hurting Sammi.

"You killed Shannon, too," I said. "Why?"

"She worked out that I borrowed some of her ingredients to make a potion," said Grace. "A potion that slows the heartbeat and mimics the appearance of death. It was hidden in one of my hair dye bottles. I should have been more careful about hiding them. I suspect your friend Alissa will have worked it out by now, but no matter."

"And you used the walking stick to kill Shannon and throw us off the trace?"

"It was too easy," said Grace. "Aveline will die in her own time. The sceptre would never have chosen her again. As it is, there's only one possible choice."

"You won't take it." I raised the sceptre like a shield, but in truth, I had no idea if it was even possible for me to wield its power. It was much heavier than a wand, and I didn't want to risk bringing the whole tomb crashing down by accident.

Instead, I went for my wand, but the three of them got there first. Three spells slammed into me, sending me flying off my feet. The sceptre clattered to the tiled floor, and Sammi made a frantic grab for it.

Grace waved her wand and my body froze, every muscle locking. Sammi stiffened, too, her hands inches from the sceptre. Her eyes bulged, her hand reaching out, but like me, she was unable to move an inch.

"I *should* finish you both off." Grace strode over to us. "But I don't need to worry about everyone knowing I stole the sceptre now. And I take no pleasure in killing children. Or… whatever you are, Blair."

Her hand closed around the sceptre. *No.*

"By the way, I have to thank you." She turned the sceptre over in her hands, as though admiring the way the purple gem on the end caught the light.

I managed to speak. "For what?"

"That werewolf potion of yours, of course," she said. "I recognised it for what it was immediately. It would have been wasted on Aveline, but it helped me prevent anyone from interfering. It even worked on the cat."

A gasp escaped. "You fed it to my cat?"

"Your cat will be fine, Blair. Pity I can't say the same for you."

She pointed the sceptre at me. The air trembled, and my frozen body screamed in terror. *Think, Blair.* Nobody would hear us cry for help. It was up to me to get us out, but there was only one exit and neither of us could move a muscle, not even to use magic.

"There's no reason to look so frightened," said Grace. "Someone will come and find you eventually, I don't doubt. But we have a job to do, so... I doubt I'll be seeing you again."

My fingers inched towards one another, bit by bit. Then with a snap, I glamoured myself invisible. Another snap and Sammi vanished, too.

Patience let out a curse. "Where did they go?"

"Must have used a spell." Grace looked at the spot where we'd vanished, scowling. "A fairy trick, maybe. Is she still there?"

I held my breath. Sammi didn't move an inch either, not that either of us *could*. But if they thought we'd escaped, they might hesitate before using the sceptre.

"What if they got out?" said Charity. "They'll go right for that meddlesome Madame Grey."

"Then we'll get to her first," said Patience. "It doesn't matter if either of them *is* still there—they won't undo that spell in a hurry. We need to catch up to the procession before the ceremony."

"We do," said Grace. "One way or another, one of us will wield the sceptre by the night's end. All that's left to do is remove Madame Grey."

The ceremony. No.

She waved her wand. There was flash of light, then all went black.

———

Glitter woke me. Glitter, and the pixie's bony finger poking me in the face. My eyes flickered open. The little pixie flitted about in front of me. I tried to reach out, but I was still immobilised.

A groan came from next to me. "Sammi?"

"Am I dead?" Sammi asked.

"No, I glamoured you."

"You did what to me?"

"Turned you invisible. It's a type of fairy illusion spell," I explained. "I hoped it would buy us time, but they left us anyway. How long was I out for?"

"I don't know." She sniffed. "I can't move."

"I can't move, either." Grace and the others were on their way to threaten Madame Grey and wreck the ceremony, and here I was stuck in a tomb and frozen on the spot. "Hey, pixie, can you undo the spell on us? Please?"

He flew down to my shoulder, making odd chittering noises. He cast a guilty look at Sammi and shook his head.

"Sammi, do you know what spell she used?"

"I think so," she mumbled. "It's a Grade Five spell. We don't learn that sort of magic for another couple of years."

"Well, it can't last forever." I twitched my fingers. "Pixie, can you please find someone to get us out? And call reinforcements. We're going to need them."

If it wasn't already too late. The three Rosemary witches didn't need to worry about hiding their goals, not now they had the sceptre. My guess was that they'd planned to murder Aveline and steal it from the start, but Sammi had got there first, forcing them to rethink their plan. But now they'd successfully taken the sceptre on Samhain, the worst possible day for it to be in the wrong hands.

"Where in the world is Vincent?" I muttered.

"Probably sleeping," said Sammi.

I tried to crane my neck to look at her. "You were at the vampires' place the other day, weren't you? Why?"

"I just wanted to ask them a few questions about summoning the dead," Sammi whispered. "Whether ghosts could hurt people, things like that. I did prepare before taking the sceptre."

"There's no such thing as too prepared when it comes to an object like that," I said. "I'm not blaming you, though. If you hadn't stolen it, Grace and her daughters would probably have killed Aveline on that first night."

"They still got it, didn't they?" There was a sob in her voice.

The door opened. I held my breath, but it wasn't one of the Rosemary witches. Instead, a witch around Sammi's age shuffled into the mausoleum. As the light fell on her face, I recognised her.

"Rebecca?" I said.

"Blair? Are you there?" She squinted into the darkness. "I can't see you."

"Right—the glamour." I snapped my fingers and turned myself and Sammi visible again. "How did you know we were here?"

"I came looking for you," Rebecca said. "When you didn't show up at the ceremony. I asked Vincent, but he said his people were asleep. He said someone spiked their blood supply with a potion."

I swore. "Grace must have slipped them the werewolf potion, too. I never would have used it if I knew it would give her ideas about how to ensure nobody stopped her plan."

It wasn't Rob's fault, either. The Rosemary witches

were resourceful, and had been prepared for any possible scenario.

Rebecca looked between me and Sammi. "Blair, did they give you the potion, too? Why are you on the floor?"

"No, they used a Grade Five freezing spell which I don't know how to undo," I said. "Neither of us can move."

Rebecca stiffened. "I—I think I know that spell. My... my mum used it on me, and I saw Blythe undo it. But I don't know if I can do it from memory."

"It's worth a shot," I said.

Rebecca's face paled. "What if I mess it up? I've never tried."

"First time for everything," I said. "Don't worry, I'm fine with being a guinea pig."

She took in a deep breath and pointed her wand at me. A flash of light ignited, and she winced. "Not quite that. Let me think..."

"Blair, are you sure you trust her?" Sammi's voice came from beside me.

"I do," I said. "Go on, Rebecca."

Her expression cleared, and she flicked her wand. At once, sensation came back into my limbs. "Nice going."

Her face brightened. "It worked?"

"It did." I straightened upright. "Can you stay here with Sammi while I catch up to the Rosemary witches? They have the sceptre. It's not safe out there for either of you."

Rebecca bit her lip. "Okay. I'll stay here."

Time was of the essence. Even Madame Grey might not be able to stop three witches with a sceptre on Samhain if she didn't know it was coming.

"Wait," Sammi blurted. "In my pocket—the book. You

might need it, if you want to deal with the sceptre. I'm not sure even the Rosemary witches have read it."

"I forgot." I held out my hand and she gave me the book I'd seen on Madame Grey's desk. "Do you have any idea what they might be planning to use it for?"

"No," whispered Sammi. "Please be careful, Blair."

Okay. I guess I'm winging it, then—literally.

I snapped my fingers, transforming into my fairy form. As the two young witches gawped at me, I flew out of the tomb and vanished.

15

I flew through the foggy cemetery. Even with wings, I collided with several headstones on my way out. The vampires' headquarters was silent. *I can't believe the Rosemary witches used that potion on the vampires.* Grace must be confident the sceptre would give her more than enough power to escape unscathed. She and her daughters had fooled everyone, even Aveline and Madame Grey. Using a potion that mimicked death would have got around all the extra spells that the police used to check whether a dead body was actually dead or not. I just hoped the pixie had kept the Rosemary witches distracted for long enough that they wouldn't reach Madame Grey before I did.

The fog had darkened as evening approached, meaning the ceremony would soon be underway. I glamoured myself invisible once I came within hearing distance of the procession on the hillside. The chatter of students filled the air, a reminder that there were a lot of innocent people here, unaware of the three vipers in their midst.

I flew through the fog, having to stay higher in the air than I'd have liked or else risk flying straight into the procession. Blurred cloaked figures appeared in the fog below. Madame Grey would be at the front of the line, but it appeared to have no end, a flood of witches and wizards smothered in endless whiteness.

Then I spotted three figures apart from the others, trekking down the hillside. The glowing purplish light of the sceptre was unmistakable. This was no hallucination in the fog, but Grace and her daughters, sneaking up on the oblivious witches and wizards gathering on the hillside. Judging by the way they carried on chatting, they had no idea they were about to be ambushed. The Rosemary witches might not have created the fog themselves, but they'd used it to their full advantage. Ghosts appeared, surrounding the three Rosemary witches as though drawn by the sceptre's presence. Shivering, I flew overhead, hoping my glamour remained in place, and pointed my wand at Grace from behind.

My spell bounced clean off her. She must have used the sceptre to shield herself—unless it was the ghosts.

Grace turned on the spot. "Don't bother hiding, Blair. I knew you'd wriggle out of our trap. You think I'm unaware of your special *fairy* powers?"

I should have known. The last thing I wanted was to show myself, but if they froze me again, they'd have total control.

"I have something I think you want." I dug my hand in my pocket for the book. "You can't use the sceptre without knowing how it works."

"You mean to bargain with us?" she said. "We know how to use the sceptre, and we don't need a guidebook to know that it will pick one of us at the end of the ceremony. We already have its power on our side. The spirits know that, too."

My heart gave a sickening dive. The sceptre was glowing in her hands, the same way it had done in Aveline's, surrounded by flickering spirits.

Did that mean it was already too late?

"What are you going to do to Aveline?" I said. "It still belongs to her by right."

"Not for much longer." She held the sceptre high. "Let's see how Madame Grey deals with this."

The thickening fog turned solid, and my wings stopped mid-beat as though caught in a net. But the spell had a worse effect on the crowd. The procession ground to a halt as the fog pressed on them from either side, a solid force caging them in position.

I heard Aveline's shout drifting over the crowd. I beat my wings, attempting to fly towards her. It was like moving through thick mud, but inch by inch, I drew closer. Aveline hobbled along, muttering angrily to herself.

"Hey!" I shouted at her. "Stop the line. You're walking into a trap."

"What are you blathering on about, girl?" she said.

"Grace Rosemary faked her death, and she has the sceptre. She and her daughters are controlling this fog and they're planning to claim the sceptre's magic for their own. They killed Shannon and they're coming for you next."

"Don't be ridiculous, girl," she said. "Nobody but me can use the sceptre."

"Not for much longer." My wings beat so hard they hurt, and the fog continued to press against me like a solid force. The air was as thick as sludge

Several disgruntled shouts echoed down the line. Nobody could see where they were going, but they hadn't broken into a panic yet. They didn't know the worsening fog was the result of a spell.

"Believe me, Grace isn't dead," I said. "She has the sceptre right there—"

Grace appeared, parting the fog with a blast of violet light.

Aveline turned her way, her eyes widening. "She really is alive."

"You don't say." *How can I stop this?* Even wings weren't much of an advantage against the fog or the ghosts, let alone the sceptre.

Aveline grabbed for her wand, as did several others who were quick on the uptake, but their spells bounced off a solid wave of ghosts cloaking the three Rosemary witches, preventing anyone from touching them.

"Stop!" screamed a voice. A blast of air flew at the three witches from behind, smacking into the shield.

Sammi appeared behind them, running down the hillside. Oh, *no.* She must have left Rebecca and followed me in an attempt to make up for stealing the sceptre—but one novice witch was no match for three dangerous killers. I tried to catch her eye, but she wasn't looking at me.

Rebecca appeared behind Sammi, panting hard.

"STOP!" she screamed at the three witches.

Amazingly, they did. The shielding spell hadn't blocked her powers—but she'd never used it on three people before, let alone three adult witches wielding a powerful magical object.

"Get out of the way!" she yelled at Sammi. "I don't know how long it will last."

"I can't move!" Sammi said. "The ghosts—Blair, help me!"

I beat my wings as hard as I could, but it was hopeless —while the Rosemary witches might be trapped by Rebecca's magic, the fog and the spirits remained, keeping the rest of us held in place.

Then a flash of glittering light drew my eyes. The pixie flitted past… and he wasn't alone.

A flock of other winged creatures flew alongside him in a flood of light. The ghosts cringed backwards from the brightness, and even Grace shielded her eyes against the wings' reflective light. The pixie had brought friends.

A cry from Sammi alerted me to the sceptre in Grace's hands. I flew through the thinning fog as a flood of pixies descended on her. The sceptre dropped from her hands, rolling down the hillside.

Several people grabbed for it at once, but Rebecca got there first. Her hands closed around the sceptre's base, and a cry escaped her as it lit up with a dazzling purple light.

"NO!" screamed Grace. "I won't allow it."

Rebecca straightened upright, the sceptre in her hands, looking bewildered. "What do I do with it?"

"The sceptre has chosen you," Aveline said. "You're the next Head Witch."

Rebecca swayed on the spot as though she was about to faint. With an impatient noise, the former Head Witch flicked her wand, sending all three Rosemary witches sprawling into the mud.

Before she could do more, Madame Grey herself swept towards us, waving her wand. In an instant, the three Rosemary witches lay in a heap, their hands and ankles bound.

The crowd looked on, dumbstruck at the sight of the sceptre in Rebecca's hands.

"Is this a trick?" said Sammi. "It can't have chosen her. I mean, she's a kid, right?"

"It's never happened before," said Madame Grey. "But the sceptre's choice cannot be doubted."

Rebecca trembled the spot, her face pale. "No way."

"She's right," Grace called from the ground. "No way. It's a mistake. We didn't even finish the ceremony. Try again and it'll pick one of us for sure."

Rebecca swung the sceptre around, pointing it directly at them. "It won't pick any of you. You're liars and murderers."

"The message is clear," Madame Grey put in. "The sceptre stays here in Fairy Falls."

Silence fell. Then applause rippled through the crowd as the witches and wizards caught on to what was happening.

"Rebecca Dailey!" The voices rang out in a chorus. Hats flew into the air in a flurry, caught in their owners' hands.

Rebecca stared at the crowd calling her name, lost for words, as I landed at her side.

"Don't worry," I whispered. "Madame Grey will help you."

I hoped so, because I was clueless. But the murderers lay tied up at our feet, the fog was clearing, and a flock of glittering wings passed overhead before disappearing from sight.

16

The morning after Samhain, I woke bright and early and determined to join Alissa and restore my flat to its previous condition. The first item on our agenda was to replace that ghastly pink sofa with our old comfy furniture. Sky's contribution was to wander around and leave cat hair on everything, meowing at the top of his lungs. I was so relieved to have my purring familiar back again that I didn't even mind when he destroyed the last piece of bubble wrap he found under the bed.

"I'm glad you're okay," I whispered, stroking him behind the ears.

"Miaow." Sky seemed oddly subdued, perhaps because he'd been left out of the Samhain ceremony after suffering through so many rehearsals. He hissed in Aveline's direction when she stomped into the room, looking at the restored furniture arrangement with a disgruntled expression on her face.

"You might have waited until I was gone before you set your little monsters loose in here," she said.

"We're not running a hostel, Aveline," Alissa said, ducking out of her bedroom with a purring Roald in her arms. Leaning close to me, she whispered, "He peed in her bed last night."

I stifled a laugh at the furious expression on Aveline's face. Before she could lash out, Vanessa came into view.

"Oh, Blair, Alissa." She gave us a watery smile. "Thank you for your hospitality."

"Sorry your stay wasn't a pleasant one," I said. "And for the ghosts, the thievery and the murders."

"Miaow," said Sky, which might have meant, *and for the cat hair.* Or it could have meant, *go away.* He'd made his feelings on us ever having anyone to stay in the flat again crystal clear.

Thanks to Madame Grey, the Rosemary witches were on their way to jail where they belonged, while Aveline intended to take her daughter back home and enjoy her retirement in peace. She'd had a more eventful trip than planned, and despite her behaviour, I felt kind of sorry for the way her reign as Head Witch had ended.

"Someone's here to see you," Vanessa said, peering out the window.

An instant later, the doorbell rang. *Nathan?* He'd been on the night shift again, preventing me from talking to him face to face about last night's events. No doubt he'd heard it all—everything I hadn't been able to fit into a text message, anyway.

It wasn't Nathan. I opened the front door to find Rebecca outside, holding the sceptre in her hand like a giant baton that made her look even younger than usual.

Behind me, Aveline came out of the room, and Rebecca shot her a nervous glance.

"Hey," I said. "How's it going?"

"Uh, fine." She bit her lip, glancing at Aveline again. "I'm sorry. For using my power on you."

She grunted. "You have a gift, girl. A dangerous one. See to it that you listen to your mentor in future."

Rebecca blinked in surprise. "I'm not ready for this," she blurted. "You're a more experienced witch than I am. I can barely use a wand, let alone the sceptre."

"Experience?" she said. "You have more experience than most witches your age, I'd wager. Ignore the naysayers. It never did me any harm."

I raised an eyebrow. Treating people's houses like hostels was a step too far, but Rebecca had way more sense than a lot of adults I'd met. The former Head Witch being one of them.

"But I have no idea how to use it," she mumbled.

"Do you think I did when I was first chosen as the bearer?" said Aveline. "Just point it in the direction of your enemies and you'll be fine."

I opened my mouth to berate her for encouraging Rebecca to make enemies, then closed it. Besides, the way Rebecca's face lit up was almost worth the last week of indignity.

Almost.

"How was it with Sammi?" I asked her.

She shrugged. "She apologised."

"You might find you understand one another better now." The whole thing might turn out to be a learning experience for all of them. Even if not, with the sceptre in her hand, her classmates would think twice before challenging her in future.

She nodded. "I guess. Thanks, Blair."

Vanessa walked into the hallway, her eyes taking in the sceptre with evident disappointment. "So it did choose you. A child as Head Witch? How can this be?"

"Better than a murderer," I said.

"The girl's right, for once," Aveline said. "The sceptre's just a ceremonial piece. You won't need to use it most of the time."

"You used it to put your shoes on," Vanessa pointed out. "And to clean the kitchen. And…"

"Yes, but I'm older," said Aveline. "And more experienced. You would have been a terrible Head Witch."

Vanessa dropped the suitcase she was holding. "Maybe I never wanted the title to begin with, mother. Perhaps I wanted it out of *your* hands so you couldn't use your power to belittle me."

"If you're going to argue, don't do it in our hallway," Alissa called.

Sky chose that moment to wander out of my room and transform into a huge fuzzy monster. Vanessa took one look at him and stumbled backwards. Eyes wide, she grabbed the suitcase and hauled it out of the hall, fleeing the house with her mother yelling obscenities behind her.

When they turned back at the front gate to make sure Sky wasn't following them, he resembled a cat again, sitting on the doorstep and licking a paw.

"You were saving that, weren't you?" I whispered to him.

"Miaow." He planted himself in front of the door as though daring either of them to come back in.

Fighting a grin, I turned to Rebecca. "You okay?"

"Sure." She hesitated, then dropped her voice. "Blair, I'm told today is the last day. To contact the dead. I mean, if you wanted to speak to your mother…"

My heart dip-dived. "She's not buried in the grave-yard. I checked."

"I know," Rebecca said. "I—my mother mentioned a cottage in the woods. I think it's where she lived."

"In the woods?" I echoed. "Are you sure?"

Her shoulders hunched. "Yes. She said it's near the elves' territory, on the west side of the woods."

My mother lived in the woods? It would explain why my dad had ended up on the elves' territory when he'd been on the run, and why I'd never run into anyone who knew where Tanith Wildflower had spent her time when she'd lived here.

"I'm sorry I didn't tell you before," she said quickly. "I didn't know—I mean, we thought your mum was alive, and then she wasn't, and—"

"No worries." I put on a false smile, genuinely grateful. "I'd like to at least try."

Yesterday, I'd seen fairies fly from some other world into this one. I'd seen spirits rise to speak to the living. While the number of ghostly encounters was rumoured to have slowed overnight, I wouldn't get another chance.

———

Rebecca and I walked through the town in silence. Despite the sceptre's size, she held it in a firm grip and kept her head high, no doubt as Madame Grey had instructed her to do. On my other side walked Sky, while

197

Toast accompanied his witch, purring nonstop. He didn't seem put off by the sceptre at all.

We passed the hospital on our way to the path leading into the forest. Briefly, I wondered if old Ava knew Tanith Wildflower's address, too. If she did, it didn't matter. I just hoped I hadn't left it too late.

We meandered down the path into the woods, skirting the elves' territory. No sound pursued us except the chatter of birdsong and our own footsteps. Sky was the first to turn off the path, jerking his tail towards a half-collapsed fence surrounded by trees.

On the other side of the fence sat a small cottage. The garden was overgrown and unkempt, while the cottage itself had fallen into disrepair. The windows were matted in cobwebs, several roof tiles were missing, and the door rotted in its frame.

Sky meowed and brushed against my ankles in a show of support. I stroked him behind the ears and opened the creaky old gate into the garden. Rebecca followed, looking around nervously.

My mother must have liked growing herbs, by the look of the overgrown garden. Fragrant smells surrounded the house, making my nose itch. I peered through the windows, but the house was as abandoned as it looked. Silence hung over it, as thick as the scent of herbs.

"Where do you want me to do the spell?" Rebecca whispered.

"Here in the garden will do." I halted in the middle of an unkempt patch of grass. My pulse fluttered as I knelt down and laid out the herbs in the same pattern as I had when I'd summoned Shannon's ghost.

Rebecca held out the sceptre over the herbs and muttered under her breath.

Then I whispered, "I want to speak to Tanith Wildflower."

A thin layer of fog sprang up at my words, flowing from the sceptre until it solidified into a human-like figure. Rebecca let out a soft exclamation.

As for me... I froze. The person standing before me looked almost solid. Medium height, long curly dark hair, pale skin.

She looked like me. Tears sprang to my eyes and flowed over.

"Oh, Briar, don't cry," she whispered.

"It's Blair," I mumbled. "Briar... is that the name you gave me?"

Old Ava had called me Briar, on more than one occasion. *Briar Wildflower*. Would that have been my name?

My mother floated down, her feet touching the ground as though she was alive, not separated from me by the barrier between the dead and the living.

"I did," she said. "I knew they wouldn't keep the name when I gave you away. It tore me apart, but your father and I had no choice in the matter. Have you... have you had a good life, at least?"

Where to start? I'd lived with three different foster families before I was three. Mr and Mrs Wilkes, meanwhile, were as oblivious to my magical state as it was possible to be. And yet I'd still found my way into the magical world. I wasn't the same person who'd obliviously wandered into Fairy Falls.

"Yeah." I blinked hard, several times. "I have. And they called me Blair. My foster parents, I mean. They're great, but they're not… paranormal. Why did you leave me outside the magical world?"

You were never meant to be part of this world, Mr Harker had said. And he hadn't lied. That's what *he'd* believed, but despite knowing he was trying to hurt me, his words had wormed their way into my head.

My breath caught as my mother's ghost moved closer, close enough for her finger to brush against my chin. "I wish I could have had you raised in the magical world, but Fairy Falls is built on secrets. I feared for you, especially given… your father."

"You mean, because I'm half fairy." My throat tightened. "I wouldn't give this up for anything."

"I know, Blair," she said. "I'd feel the same in your position. You wouldn't have been safe in this world during your childhood. I should have left you some direction so you'd be able to follow us, but I feared the information would fall into the wrong hands. Your father thought the same."

"You know he's in jail, right?" I asked. "I—it was only a few years ago, so you died before then. Aveline Hollyhock said you stole the sceptre. Is it true?"

"It's true."

My lie-sensing power echoed her words.

My heart contracted. "Why?"

"Because our lives were in danger, Blair," she whispered. "The sceptre would have bought us time, but not enough. We had the hunters on our tail. It broke me to leave you behind, but what else could I do? At least if I left you of my own volition, I might be able to find you again… had I lived. Blair, the hunters are more dangerous than you know."

"My dad keeps telling me the same thing. He sends me notes from jail—from the LFPF. Please—tell me. Did they kill you?"

Nathan's father had said that he'd found her already dying, so it wasn't him, but someone had left her for dead. Left her for the hunters to find.

"The fairies, Blair," she said, her voice growing fainter. "Don't trust them—never trust them."

"The fairies killed you?" I lurched to my feet, but she grew fainter. The merest brush of air whispered against my cheek and then she was gone.

"No," I said. "I summon you, Tanith Wildflower."

I spoke her name again, and again, but she didn't reappear.

"The light's gone out, Blair," Rebecca said from behind me. "I'm sorry."

I sank to the ground, tears stinging my eyes, and turned back to face the cottage. The place my family—half of it, at least—had lived.

The place I'd have grown up, if not for the fairies. If not for the hunters, who'd driven my mother out of her home.

I'd seen her once and found out her side of the story. My dad would provide the rest. And then? I'd find a way to bring the truth to light, and free him for jail.

I promise.

Vowing to keep my word, I turned away from my mother's home, towards the brightening sky.

ABOUT THE AUTHOR

Elle Adams lives in the middle of England, where she spends most of her time reading an ever-growing mountain of books, planning her next adventure, or writing. Elle's books are humorous mysteries with a paranormal twist, packed with magical mayhem.

She also writes urban and contemporary fantasy novels as Emma L. Adams.

Find Elle on Facebook at https://www.facebook.com/pg/ElleAdamsAuthor/